Also by Sarah Moss

FICTION

Summerwater

Ghost Wall

The Tidal Zone

Signs for Lost Children

Bodies of Light

Night Waking

Cold Earth

NONFICTION

Names for the Sea: Strangers in Iceland

Chocolate: A Global History
(coauthored with Alec Badenoch)

*Spilling the Beans: Eating, Cooking,
Reading and Writing in British Women's Fiction,
1770–1830*

THE FELL

THE FELL

Sarah Moss

FARRAR, STRAUS AND GIROUX

NEW YORK

Farrar, Straus and Giroux
120 Broadway, New York 10271

Printed in the United States of America
Originally published in 2021 by Picador, Great Britain
Published in the United States by Farrar, Straus and Giroux
First American edition, 2022

Library of Congress Cataloging-in-Publication Data
Names: Moss, Sarah, author.
Title: The Fell / Sarah Moss.
Description: First American edition. | New York : Farrar, Straus and Giroux, 2022.
Identifiers: LCCN 2021044930 | ISBN 9780374606046 (hardcover)
Classification: LCC PR6113.O88 F45 2022 | DDC 823/.92—dc23
LC record available at https://lccn.loc.gov/2021044930

Our books may be purchased in bulk for promotional,
educational, or business use. Please contact your local bookseller or
the Macmillan Corporate and Premium Sales Department at 1-800-221-7945,
extension 5442, or by email at MacmillanSpecialMarkets@macmillan.com.

www.fsgbooks.com
www.twitter.com/fsgbooks • www.facebook.com/fsgbooks

1   3   5   7   9   10   8   6   4   2

THE FELL

nerve endings

I THINK IT'S ready, Ellie says. Her hair, pale, silky, swings over her face as she peers into the oven. You get the plates, Dad. You'll need the oven gloves, Rob hears himself say, and she sighs, as he knew she would. No, really, I thought it would be more fun to get like sixth-degree burns and spend the next four hours screaming in agony in the waiting room at A and E. Fourth degree, he says, there's nothing after that.

Fourth-degree burns go through skin and underlying tissue to muscle and bone, and are usually painless because the nerve endings are destroyed. You wouldn't get them from picking up an oven tray. He doesn't say that. Also, even under current conditions a child with fourth- or even third-degree burns would be seen immediately, though however bad the injury he'd drive her to hospital because ambulance response times are buggered. He doesn't say that either. The oven gloves need a wash. Will you have my mushrooms and give me your olives, Ellie says,

3

sliding the pizza perfectly competently from the tray to the plate, using the oven gloves to put the tray into the sink where it hisses a little. He likes olives. Of course I will, love, he says. It's his weekend for giving her whatever she wants, except that they've only just swapped toppings, he's only about to take the first bite, when his phone goes, and he knows before he looks, because it always happens when you don't want it to – as well as sometimes when you do – which call it is, and he knows he could say no, you can always say no, and he knows he won't, because you never do, not unless you've drunk too much to drive which he hasn't because he never does, not these days. She looks at him, at the phone vibrating on the counter, threatening to jump, and he walks away from her as he picks it up.

the fourteen days

MATT STANDS BACK to the wall, on the corner, safety off and fingers on the trigger. He won't see nightfall but he's going to take Jake down with him if no one else. That fucker. The air around him sucks in, a change in pressure that's also a sound, and then the bridge at the end of the street implodes gracefully, as if a black hole opened in the river below and pulled it in. Dust boils into the dimming sky. It's never fully light here. You can never see far enough. There are no shadows to warn you of what's coming – and here he is, right now; Matt takes aim, waits until the crosshairs are on his friend's chest, pisses a stream of ammo into Jake as he feels his own strength fade.

He sits back, rolls his shoulders. The light's changed. He really needs to pee. He's hungry. He reaches for his phone and messages Jake. Later, yeah? Gotta go. He picks up the phone and on second thoughts leaves it on his desk. It doesn't have to be in the same room as him, not

5

all the time. He's not dependent. There's something weird going on with his neck when he stands up. He winces, stretches until stuff clunks.

It's when he comes downstairs that he realises he's the only one in the house. The cat's sitting on the stairs, waiting, the way that she does when there's nothing going on. He's always thought it would be useful at school, to be able to switch yourself off like that, to be either so deep in thought that the total lack of event in your immediate environment is hardly noticeable or so dim that it doesn't bother you, not that being dim seems to help people tolerate school. When he used to leave in the mornings he often wanted to swap with the cat, spend the day dozing and eating and trotting off to menace other cats in the garden, let the cat sit through assembly and Maths, see how long it takes anyone to notice. There's a stillness in the house he hasn't known for weeks, a sense of space that used to be normal after school or if Mum was out in the evening, the place to himself to play his music and fry eggs and cheese sandwiches and sometimes boxes of frozen burgers from the village shop without her on at him to open the windows and wash up before he's even eaten and she doesn't understand how he can not think about the cows and the workers in the abattoir who all get PTSD because you would, wouldn't you, killing animals all day, not to mention if people didn't eat meat we wouldn't be in this mess in the first place and can't he at least put the extractor fan on. Hope rises for a moment, that he can maybe at least make a toastie and put some music on, not that he can't do those things when she's around but he could do them better, more peacefully, if she's out, though of course she can't be out, not even for a walk, not for another six days, seven hours and twenty minutes. Give or take. The fourteen days, he heard her ask on the phone, what time does it end, is it noon or midnight or from when I last saw my colleague, which would have been about five o'clock on Thursday? She'll be in the garden, must have managed to go out there and get on with something instead of wandering in and out the way she has the last few days, starting what she calls tidying up only the effect is more like messing up and five minutes later stopping to water the plants or put the wash on but not finishing anything and then she can't find the watering can because she left it on the windowsill, and she put the laundry in the machine two days ago but didn't start it so now they're out of towels and she can't have a bath, which is what she used to do to relax when she was all wound up after a gig or tired after a long shift at the café. Use a dirty one, he said, having never really seen why towels that by definition have been used only to dry newly washed skin can be dirty. You don't have a bath and then use a dirty towel, she said, and anyway we don't have money to waste on the hot water, it doesn't matter. He started the machine – they're low on washing powder –

and decided he'll just deal with the laundry himself for now. He saw her out by the shed before breakfast yesterday, skipping, like with an actual skipping rope, one he vaguely remembers from years ago with blue-painted smiley-face handles, still in her pyjamas and no socks with her trainers, hair and – other things – bouncing, and she kept getting it wrong, tangling and tripping, until she threw the rope across the patio and thumped her own head with her fists. He knew when the call came that he'd be fine, two weeks of lie-ins and gaming, no sweat, not as if the weather this time of year makes you want to go out anyway even if there was anywhere to go, and he knew it would be harder for her but you don't expect, he didn't expect, to see your mum basically losing it, hours spent pacing from the front gate through the house to the bottom of the garden and back, followed by the cat who is interested by people coming in and going out and apparently gratified to have the process on repeat. Try an on-line workout, he said, I'll help you move the coffee table. You could make bread, couldn't you, or try knitting again. I know, she kept saying, I know, I should, I just can't bear – I don't think I've ever spent a whole day inside in my life. You must have done, he said, you've been ill, haven't you? What about when I was born? But neither of them can remember her being ill, not enough to stay in bed, and she says that actually she spent most of her labour with him under an apple tree in the garden of

Dad's parents' house, that it was helpful to hang on to the branches. Yeah, he said, ew, thanks Mum, so do some more gardening, you know you're allowed in the garden as long as you don't come within two metres of the neighbours and they won't be out there this time of year. I know, she said, I'm making a fuss, I just find this really hard, I knew I would. Not, he thought, as hard as getting sick, not as hard as Deepak's dad who was in Intensive Care for three weeks or the grandparents of kids in his class who've died this year or his Maths teacher who's back at work but can't get enough breath for a sentence half the time, compared to that doing the garden instead of going up the fells is actually quite manageable, so how about he games and she does yoga in the garden and they hope neither of them starts with the fever and loss of taste and smell. He takes the mustard from the fridge, opens the jar to make sure he can still smell it, which he can even though there's barely a scrape left. He's going to make that toastie, and if she comes in and starts on about washing up and not eating everything when they can't get to the shops he'll just make one for her, quarter it on a plate with a sliced apple the way she likes, say nothing. There are crumbs underfoot, he can feel them sticking to his socks. He'll even sweep the floor, once he's eaten. He butters the last few slices of bread, finds there isn't really enough cheese either but it'll have to do, sets the pan to warm and goes up to get his phone for something to look at while he eats.

He starts his music, hearing it properly and not through his crappy cheap earbuds for the first time in days, though come to think of it Mum hasn't been playing her own stuff either. He turns it up and then remembers that Samira next door is working nights and turns it down again. The cat sits on the counter and watches as he puts his plate in the dishwasher, singing along, drinks the last of the milk out of the carton and rinses it and puts it in the recycling, plastic lid and cardboard separated the way Mum likes. He might, he thinks, even wash the frying pan, while the music plays, but he leaves it in the sink for now, where there's a puddle of tea leaves over the plug. It's not as if Mum's perfect herself, she must know the tea leaves don't go down the drain and actually you don't want them to, which doesn't mean you want them sitting there, someone's going to have to deal with it, aren't they? He taps the strainer into the compost bin, which is overflowing with tea and onion skins and apple cores because it always is. He's not going to deal with that now either – if she's in the garden he's all for leaving her there in peace – but he does fold the laundry he hung yesterday on the rack positioned against the radiator even though Mum still hasn't turned the heating on. Let's see if we can hold out even into December, she says, what with how warm it is now, we used to get the first frosts in September, do you remember? And though he usually points out that the relationship between the name of the month and the indoor temperature of a limestone terraced house halfway up a hill in the Peak District is at best variable, usually doesn't point out that he knows they can't afford the heating and she doesn't have to jolly him along, so far she's been more or less right. The heavier clothes, his jeans and her hoody, aren't exactly dry but close enough, wearing them would be bad only for the first few minutes. Four of seven socks are hers, how is he still losing socks when he hasn't left the house for a week? He slings his own stuff over his shoulder, drapes hers over the other arm, takes it all upstairs escorted by the cat.

He doesn't like seeing Mum's room so tidy. He thinks of her fridge magnet *A Tidy House is the Sign of an Empty Mind*. She's been making her bed every morning this week, which never used to happen, spreading out the patchwork quilt that's lived in the bottom of the wardrobe since Grandma died, leaving one of Grandma's lumpy tapestry cushions on the pillow, after all the times she found him watching those house renovation programmes and asked him why people put cushions and covers on beds just to come back sixteen hours later and take them off again. How would he know about cushions, it's the architecture he likes, the way the architect imagines what doesn't exist but it's not like drawing or films or even most games where you can make light without shade or muck about with gravity, the maths and physics have to work and the architects have to think of materials that do what they want or think of what they

want to do with the materials they've got and there's
something about that he loves, the limits and the invent-
ing and then seeing it made in real life. He hasn't said it
to anyone, might not say it to anyone, but maybe he'll
find out how you learn to do architecture, though it's
probably a university thing and he's not sure about that,
the debt and all those years and not many kids from his
school go and he's probably not clever enough anyway—
The pile of clothes by Mum's window, things not clean
enough to put away and not dirty enough to wash, is
just the striped woolly jumper and the scarf Kiran knit-
ted for her. He dumps the clean clothes on her bed,
glances out at the garden but he can't see her, must be
doing something in the shed, potting seeds or whatever,
has to be a winter job because you plant them out in
spring. Come on then, he says to the cat, but she's arranging herself on the bed and ignores him. Wind blows
through the ash tree outside, through the leaky window to his skin. Houses need to breathe, Mum says, who
wants to live in a sealed box?

His own room is not tidy. You don't have to look, he
says, if you don't like it, that's why I keep the door closed.
You keep the door closed, she says, so I can't be judgey
about your games. Well it doesn't work then, does it, he
says, and then they have the one where she says how games
turn you into a psychopath and he says young men have
always engaged in ritual violence and would she rather he

was getting brain damage in a boxing ring or hunting with spears in the woods and she says spears in the woods, definitely, at least you'd get some fresh air and exercise. He puts his socks in the drawer, squashes everything down so he can close it, takes off the jeans he's wearing and puts on the clean ones to dry them with his body-heat before they develop that smell. He checks his phone. May as well go back to the game, but he doesn't feel like it. He might actually do some Maths, work through the textbook a bit. You have to pretend you think the exams will happen, that you're going to get qualifications and a job, you'd go mad else. He balances the keyboard on the hard drive purring at his feet and pushes some stuff to the side of his desk, finds his textbook and then his calculator under some of the stuff. He needs the light on. It's not as if it would be out of character for Mum to stay out gardening in the dark, she often goes night-walking. She used to take him out before bed when he was little, into the woods to see badgers and up the hill for stars, not that she can go into the woods or up the hill at the moment. Everything's different, she says, in the dark, you hear better, you realise it's not all about what you can see. She'll just be out there watching the dusk. Listening to the dusk. And raking leaves, or whatever, still.

air-kissing

THERE'S A QUIET on the wind, she sings, there's a silence in the air, name it if you dare, yeah, name it if you care. Silent spring, silent spring. Alice catches a glimpse of herself reflected in the framed map on the wall. Oh, so what? She boogies around a kitchen chair, dips to peer into the oven. The cookies want another minute. Funny how Janie Maddock — very young Janie Maddock, all cheekbones and ironed hair — giggles at the end of what you'd think is a protest song but is weirdly sweet and chirpy. Oh, and now Daniel Silvermann, Alice isn't sure she feels like this, you can't dance to Daniel Silvermann. I remember you there with the rose in your hair. Wasn't there a story about someone holding a gun to his head to make him sing in tune, and he still couldn't? Makes sense, really, you wouldn't sing off-key on purpose even without the gun. I remember you laughed at the flames. Lugubrious, that's the word. Skip! Springsteen, she can dance to that all right. She saw him live once, London, early seventies, she

15

was pregnant with Susie and secretly worried that some-how the loud music would harm the baby but she knew Mark would make her feel stupid if she said anything and she did want to go. Born to Run! Cookies, there's less than a minute between perfect and crunchy, if you're going to eat all that butter and sugar it better be good. Not that she is going to eat all that butter and sugar – well, maybe a couple after dinner, with a very moderate spoonful of ice cream – doesn't seem to have occurred to the government that the Extremely Vulnerable will be Extra Specially Extremely Vulnerable after months without outdoor exercise, dancing's not going to burn off many cookies. She's going to send them Special Delivery tomorrow morning, the cookies, ask Matt next door to take them to the post office and give him a few for his trouble, he can always use some feeding up, Kate keeps him on rabbit food. Not that they haven't been very kind, both of them, all the way through this, doing her shopping when she couldn't get a delivery and recently they've been walking or on bikes, even with the milk and tins, coming up the hill. The car insurance ran out, Kate said when she asked, and it's not as if we're going anywhere anyway, only she couldn't ask them for the things she really wants, salt and vinegar Hula Hoops and the expensive Bittermints, not with Kate working at Shoots and Leaves and growing her own lentils or whatever, probably hasn't eaten a Hula Hoop in decades. It's infantilising, that's what it is, having to have other people bring you food. Not that it isn't probably good for her, to feel a bit policed, borrow a sense of shame since her own seems weaker by the day and after all why shouldn't she have crisps and chocolate if she wants them, all those years of watching her weight and she still got cancer, it's not as if anyone cares now if a woman who never leaves her house weighs nine stone or ten. Or ten and a half. At least she's not drinking, or only the occasional sherry at weekends, have to mark the days somehow. Mm, this is a good batch. They're so much nicer fresh. Just one more, that big one with all the chocolate. The good thing about baking – apart from being able to send home-made treats to the grandchildren she hasn't seen for months, of course – is that they can't count her biscuit consumption, Matt can't, for example, remark to Kate that she's getting through two packets a week and half a pound of chocolate all on her own, not that he notices or cares, probably, not that a teenaged boy doesn't have better things to think about than his neighbour's diet. It's just that since Mark died she's got used to privacy, buying what she fancies – which actually used to be mostly pots of soup and remarkably expensive bread from the nice deli by the station – and eating it when she likes and none of anyone else's business, no need for ancestral voices in her head scolding about making her own soup which obviously she could, did for years, and now doesn't, so there. She'd probably better go into another room while the cookies cool. Or put the rack in the sitting room, that's a better idea, while she clears up. Newspaper on the coffee table in case of crumbs – oh hell but they're in isolation, aren't they, Matt and Kate, what do they call it, self-isolating, one of those horrible new nonsensical phrases. Social distancing, whoever came up with that, there's not much that's less social than acting as if every-one's unclean and dangerous, though the problem of course is that they are, or at least some of them are and there's no way of knowing. Medical distance, they should call it, or why not just safe distance, and when did 'dis-tance' become a verb? Language is also infected. Return, George Orwell, England has need of thee. So Matt can't go to the post office tomorrow, and the grandchildren won't get the cookies, and it's Matt's friend not Matt coming over on Friday with her shopping. Nice lad, turns out, though he looks – well, a bit dodgy, really, hood up and eyes down but she should know better than that, to judge by appearances, only appearances are a choice, aren't they, he could decide to look less – anyway, he can take some cookies too, she hates the way they won't let her pay them or do anything at all really. Very generous, of course, but there's a limit to how grateful you want to be, how help-less you want to feel, and she passed it a while ago. I was a whole person, she wants to say, I worked my way up, managed a team and a budget, I volunteered, in this and that, most of my life, I was bossy and still could be, given anyone to boss. Extremely Vulnerable. Laura says bossy is gendered, no one calls a man bossy, they either take it for granted that men are like that or they say authoritative or a good leader. She picks up another cookie, some days you have to take comfort where you find it. Puts the kettle on for a cup of tea to go with it.

She wanders over to the window. How did she forget that? Poor Matt and especially poor Kate, she'll be going mad shut up in the house. She forgot because it was just a text message, that's why, because your mind and memory can't get much purchase on pixels on a screen, because nothing feels real any more. That's probably why she's baking, to make something that wasn't there before, so there's a new thing in her house. Making friends with a biscuit, she's going to be befriending mice at this rate, like a prisoner in an old story, and it's the time of year, isn't it, the mice come in from the cold. Lots of people are getting dogs, worrying the sheep all summer and leaving mess everywhere, the farmers fuming though farmers do fume, their natural state, too much time alone, probably, and no rest, but they're quite right about the sheep and it'll be worse come lambing time, doesn't bear thinking about, what a dog will do to a field of pregnant ewes and panicky lambs. She leans her face against the glass, to feel it cold and hard. No one's touched her in months, not since she had that last lunch with Sheila back in March at the garden centre and they did the air-kissing thing they learnt late in life. No one's ever going to do that again, are they? Maybe she'll die without ever touching another human, maybe she's had her last hug, handshake, air-kiss. She realised – at the funeral, in fact, standing there singing next to Susie – that she'd almost certainly had the last sex of her life, she's come to terms with that, mostly, sorts herself out when she needs it, but you can't hug yourself or pat your own shoulder. Well, the shoulder – no, that doesn't work at all. Oh shut up, she thinks, pull yourself together, here you are warm and comfortable in your nice house with your nice neighbours arranging for their nice friends to bring you nice food and there are people dying out there, children hungry and women locked up with men who beat them and nurses working twenty-eight hours a day, you just shut up. And wash up. Stop patting yourself and put those cookies somewhere you're not going to eat them all. More Springsteen, there's a reason they don't write protest anthems about well-off retired people feeling a bit sad. What is it they say, check your privilege, and there it is, her privilege, in plain sight as always. But she's still leaning against the window, watching her breath mist the glass, thinking outrageously that at least the condensation is material evidence that she's alive, is in a body making heat and carbon dioxide – as if baking cookies weren't better evidence – when she sees Kate coming down the garden path next door, glancing left and right before she opens the gate, and striding off up the lane. Hiking boots, backpack, no pretending she's just taking a breath of air or rushing to the doctor, even supposing you're allowed to see a doctor while self-isolating. I should stop her, Alice thinks, she's breaking the law, but Kate's moving fast and Alice just stands there, cheek to cheek with her window, watching.

small blood footprints

KATE LEANS AGAINST the French windows. She's been doing that a lot, lately, leaning on walls, as if for comfort or maybe to see if they're still standing, still not letting her through. The ash tree bows to the wind and falling leaves spatter the glass. No birds, though she refilled the feeders this morning. Matt's been upstairs for a while now but the bad smell is still curling through the kitchen; it's the problem with having the bathroom back here, the original arrangement, but actually the original arrangement was probably much worse because there's no way Victorian quarry owners wasted indoor plumbing on labourers' cottages, what's now the bathroom would have been a scullery or coalshed even. She does think about them sometimes, the original inhabitants, the stirring of porridge and pottage where she now fries tofu and grills peppers but also stirs bean soup of the sort they'd surely have eaten with probably the same vegetables from the same garden as those Victorian miners, grown in earth that probably still holds the nutrients of their nightsoil, the afterlives of their bodies present in her and Matt, and aren't we all just rearrangements of the same atoms, which could maybe somehow be a comforting thought but isn't, not particularly. Dust we are and to dust we shall return, well get on with it then, wouldn't it be better sometimes just to do the returning than spend your life cowering away, weeks and months ticking by like this, not as if there weren't epidemics then too, the original inhabitants, but they got on with it, didn't they, people died and they were sad but they didn't wall themselves up, they didn't stop educating the children and forbid music, the living were allowed to live if you can call it that, Victorian mining, not that they lived long but maybe length isn't how you want to measure it. Anyway the bathroom is probably against planning regulations now and most of the neighbours have extended and remodelled, covered half the gardens in plastic conservatories and utility rooms. She'd rather have a garden which is just as well considering. The smell is still here. One of the less edifying realisations of these months in the house, that Matt shits more often than you'd think compatible with good health, several times a day, but then he also seems to eat more than you'd think possible, a constant cycle of ingestion and excretion that she hasn't had to witness since he was in nappies not of course that she doesn't poo herself, not that he doesn't probably notice her own bad smells though she does have the wit to open the window first and close the door after, and she can't keep up with the shopping and cooking and more to the point the expense, of course you shouldn't resent feeding your own child but she's started to skip meals herself now they can't go to the shops. Doesn't make sense to spend the five quid for online delivery, even if she could get a slot, she can feed them for a day on that, and the freezer's running low. There's still a bit in the garden, kale and potatoes and onions, sprouts coming along, but not enough to fuel a teenager even when he's taking no exercise whatsoever, his muscles wasting away in front of a computer screen. He's here and not here, Matt, chasing Nazis around the Moscow metro system, earbuds tethering him in a place that doesn't exist, reappearing dazed to eat all the bread and cheese. What was she doing again? She forgets everything these days, stands to reason that when you deprive people of external stimulus their brains slow down, almost a survival strategy, who could bear to be running on all cylinders and locked in like this, you'd go mad, poison yourself with your own fumes. She looks around: clearing out, again, getting rid of stuff she can't bear to see any more, things that make her too sad. She doesn't need to be reminded that there used to be friends and concerts and the café, that Tom used to come over to practise and Samira would hear it and come round to listen and stay for tea, that she used to put her hair up with the comb Andy made for her from the sheep bones they found at the bottom of the waterfall and wear a nice top for work, and the customers, mostly women of a certain age, used to notice and chat about hair, what to do with it when it goes grey and how they used to have it long like hers, henna and hairpins, boring, a bit, sometimes, but she takes it all back now, the boredom, it was human contact, it was real life, she fed them and they talked and she will always remember it, the sound of conversations, a room full of words and eating, for what is a café – what was a café – but a place for pleasure, small daily pleasures of food and talk, not that she could afford cafés herself much, the occasional coffee, but they were there, she was there, and singing in pubs, she doesn't even want to remember singing in pubs, how can that ever happen again, the singing or the pubs let alone both. They turn out to have thirty-six mugs, which is at least three times the number of people they have ever had in the house at one time and those were definitely nights for glasses not mugs, and probably twelve times the number of people they will ever have in the house again, because *domestic gatherings* are *drivers of transmission*. Kate and Matt invite you to a *domestic gathering*, to a *superspreader event*, to celebrate – oh Lord, all the things that haven't been celebrated. Kate's fortieth birthday, Matt's sixteenth. Easter. Eid, for Kiran. Diwali. Chanuka, a whole world of missed feasts. She did go up to the Nine Ladies for the summer solstice, at least there's that to remember, and maybe the rules will allow it again next month and if they don't maybe she'll go anyway, because how is anyone going to get sick from walking a few miles over the moor and standing on a hillside in the wind with a handful of other people to stand apart and sing to the year's turning point, and more to the point who is going to be out there before dawn to catch her if she does, though the police were hunting people off the hills with drones a few months ago, recording footage to post on social media to 'shame' people who'd gone for a walk, playing loud accusations at them from the sky. Go home, you are breaking the law. The birds should have come for them, for the drones, can't birds take out drones? Ravens are pretty big, and clever enough. She would have thought, before, that whatever might happen abroad this isn't the kind of country where it could ever be illegal to walk the hills, until the shock of that March day the texts came, *there are new rules in force, go home now and stay indoors* – how does the government have your phone number? But you don't have to look all that far back, the mass trespass and the song, to see that the authorities have never liked to have commoners wandering the land instead of getting and selling. *The day was just ending as I was descending, down Grinesbrook just by Upper Tor.* She doesn't sing it. *When a voice cried hey you in the way keepers do, he'd the worst face that ever I saw.* Keepers, drones, police, prisons, locking up and locking down, disease aside that kind of thing must be habit-forming. Who would have imagined, a year ago, that it would be against the law to leave your house, that there'd be a police hotline for people to denounce their neighbours for going out, and folk using it too, in the village? She's not sure she can weather this, actually, come to think of it, so don't think of it. Don't think of tablets – there was only ever paracetamol in the house and she wrapped the packets in parcel tape and put them in the car during the first lockdown, so she couldn't take them all without having to remember the version of herself that had done the taping, you can't exactly stop your future self killing yourself but you can make it more difficult, require more time for reflection. Don't think of the railway line or the Edge. Not that there are many trains running now anyway, restricted service due to the current unprecedented whatever, but they can't take away the cliffs.

She dislikes many of the mugs, always has: the red and white set that were a wedding present from someone or other, the handles are the wrong shape, bass clef, cramps your fingers, she should have made Paul take them, one of the few advantages of divorce was meant to be not having to live with his crap but somehow she ended up with the dented wardrobe they'd pulled out of a skip and his mother's sideboard which takes up half the sitting room. She has to keep the mug Matt painted ten years ago at one of those paint-your-own-mug places, though it also has an unappealing handle and is never used. The Royal Jubilee one is going, and the one from school. Not, of course, that they can in fact go, she can't leave the house and the charity shops can't open and the whole bulimic system of shopping and decluttering is backed up. Oops, damn. She hates this kitchen floor as well, the cold tiles, nothing survives a fall and the shards go everywhere, she'll have to find shoes before she sweeps up and she hasn't worn shoes in days, only wellies for the garden which would track mud everywhere. Kate stands up in her cold kitchen, in the faint smell of half-digested onions and worse, and then she raises a mug in an exaggerated toast and drops it, and a second and a third, watches the fragments skitter across the wobbly quarry tiles, into the gap under the washing machine from which nothing has ever reappeared. It's not as satisfying as you'd think. Maybe if she threw them – but Kate's not a violent person, and also she can't be bothered to clear a space for throwing mugs. There's no newspaper, of course, to wrap the pieces, because she can't go even to the newsagent. Can you recycle stoneware? Into roads, or something?

She uses a paper bag saved for kitchen compost, shuffles around squatting as she tidies up, gets a shard in her finger and another in her foot, bites out the one in her finger but has to sit down to poke and squeeze the foot, her sole, she thinks, softened already by these indoor days. Best hoover before the cat comes in.

She adds the surviving mugs to the box of stuff for charity which is blocking the hall. The box holds more things she doesn't want to think about: Matt's football boots, bought new and expensive back in March, in the last few days of innocence, and now outgrown unworn, she should sell them, all sorts of people seem to manage to make money online and God knows she could use it but it's not as if she could go to the post office and she just wants them out of her sight; the black dress she used to wear for choir concerts. Some other things. It was always silly, really, full-length velvet for community centres and village churches, freezing her tits off in winter and sweaty in summer and half the time more people in the choir than the audience. She heard on the radio once about women cutting up their velvet evening gowns to make blackout curtains at the beginning of the war and she can imagine it now, party dresses brought down, spread out on the floors for sacrificial butchery in the yellow light of 1940s lightbulbs, sequins falling, no more fun for you, whatever you were looking forward to is now cancelled. Though at least there were dances in the war, weren't there, and concerts, and sex, lots of sex, at least people were allowed to see each other. It's a stupid comparison, this isn't aerial bombardment and you have to resist the English passion for imagining ourselves always in World War Two, no one else does that, and anyway she's not cutting up the dress, just making the existence of velvet dresses someone else's problem. It's hard to believe that if shops reopen there will be people imagining themselves in want of third-hand evening gowns.

Kate looks around the hall, wonders what else could go, or what else could be put in a box to go when going is possible. Not the Whitby print, she bought that herself and chose the frame, but maybe the Cézanne poster, just because you liked something in your twenties doesn't mean you have to live with it forever. Then one day she could find something new to like, if the galleries reopen go to an exhibition and buy a new print, there's one she was admiring in the window of the shop opposite the café before it closed, an artist who'd noticed the rowans by the waterfall that Kate stops to admire every time she passes. Buying it – with what, Kate? – would support living art-ists instead of adding to the Cézanne estate, though since her younger self already added to the Cézanne estate that's a dodgy argument. Or not have anything there, enjoy a white space. An off-white space, more beige, really, the colour on the walls when they bought the house, perfectly inoffensive, it seemed then, nothing worth bothering about though to be fair Paul went on a bit about repaint-ing and she couldn't see the problem, who wants, she said, to spend time looking at the walls anyway, but the more she sees it now the greater the capacity of beige to offend.

Imagine deciding to have everything the colour of mush-room soup, all very well to inherit it but having all the colours in the world on a chart and choosing that – repainting, that's a thing she and Matt could be doing, later, even together, get Matt off his screen and put some music on, only she'd need paint and you probably can't get that from charity shops though goodness knows there must be gallons of the stuff sitting in garages and attics up and down the land, going off or doesn't paint sometimes spontaneously combust, the neighbours' shed one night when she was little, looked as if the whole town was burn-ing down, orange sky and rolling smoke and fire engines all down the street but it turned out a few cans of paint and a wooden shed can create some spectacular effects under the right conditions. Alice next door might have some paint and it'll be the posh stuff if she does, she had a lot of work done a couple of years ago, a really nice new kitchen and extension, all wood and glass, marble coun-ters, no plastic for Alice, shows what these houses can look like if you've money and taste, but she mustn't go see Alice, Extremely Vulnerable though she's no doddery old thing. Or at least wasn't, before all this, we'll all be dod-dery and who knows how old before it's done, not that viruses are ever really done, the Black Death washing around Europe for centuries and still occasionally pop-ping up when people eat, is it marmots in Mongolia? Something like that. And now it's in the mink, poor bloody mink, the cruel absurdity of farming mink for their fur and turning them into disease reservoirs and slaughtering them because they're contagious but then bulldozing them into shallow pits to contaminate the groundwater, it's just so typical of humanity in the twenty-first century and it won't end there, once it's in the mink it will be the badgers and otters, those that survive the TB cull and the pesticides and gamekeepers and cars and there's no point in thinking like this, she can't do anything about any of it. Pull yourself together. If she could go for a walk, get up onto the moors – no painting, anyway, not unless she makes her own paint, which is a thought, people must have done, mustn't they, before there was B&Q and Homestore and all the other aircraft hangars congregating where one dual carriageway meets another, out of town shopping centres but they're not centres of anything, sores festering in the skinfolds of roundabouts and motorway junctions. Paul loved them, could spend hours comparing one gadget with another which would have been all right if she could have left him to it and gone up the hills but he wanted her there, showing interest, which is one of the reasons why it wasn't such a bad thing when he finally said he was sleeping with Yvonne and everything that should have happened years earlier, maybe even before Matt was born not that you regret having your kids, took place. Kate wonders what are the ingredients of whitewash and how much do they cost and can she order them online, supposing she can afford them which she can't, actually, however much it is, and meanwhile she takes down the Cézanne and leans it against the box in the hall which maybe isn't exactly progress. The mink are coming back from the dead. As the bodies decompose they pop up, probably literally, and in the photo you could see they weren't the white silky bodies in the first pictures of the cull but red, bloody, which of course they would be because you're not going to kill all the mink you were keeping for their fur and bury them with the fur still on them, are you, which means it was someone's job, though of course it was always someone's job— Those mink, she thinks, those mink are going to haunt us forever and so they damn well should, they should be leaving small blood footprints on the street corners in Copenhagen and Dublin, they should be skittering around corners as we walk down the corridors of hospitals and schools and airports, under our feet as we go downstairs in the dark, whisking in our peripheral vision for ever more.

She should make something, she thinks, that would probably help. She started a scarf with some wool that Kiran gave her but the idea of sitting still and poking needles into tiny loops makes her shudder and anyway it's already wonky and has holes. Baking? Matt could be the kind of child who comes down the stairs to the smell of home-made cake? Bit late for that and she's not sure there's any sugar. Or butter. Cheese scones, maybe, only he's probably eaten all the cheese and she doesn't much like cheese scones, dry lumps of salt and refined carbs though there are the spelt ones at the café with rosemary and goats' cheese, they're pretty good, toasted on the side of a bowl of Jo's cauliflower soup, oh even the thought of eating something she hasn't cooked, doesn't half put you off your dinner, cooking, and not so much the cooking as the thinking about cooking. She used to make jam with Matt, every October half term, a day or two picking blackberries in the lanes and then an afternoon with steam running down the windows and the pair of them watching pink foam roil in the big pan, dribbling syrup from a wooden spoon into a saucer of cold water and trying to decide if it was 'set', only most times even when they thought it was, it wasn't, and the boiling had to start again until they either gave up and had thirteen jars of blackberry syrup in the cupboard or Matt went to bed and she ladled boiling sugar around the kitchen in the early hours of the morning. Nothing wrong with blackberries in a state of nature anyway, and they freeze well enough. The last of them will be rotting on the bushes out there now, used to be half the town out picking through the autumn when she was little but nobody bothers now, rather have mangos flown around the world. She's becoming a grumpy old woman, that's what, she's even boring herself, it's going to be avocados she's complaining about next.

Her wellies lean on each other at the back door. She pulls them on, notices mud on the jeans she's been wearing – how many days? She has been doing laundry, some laundry, it's not as if she and Matt aren't changing their pants, though she gave up on bras early on, just another thing to wash. That's something else she could get rid of, though even someone in principle willing to consider a second-hand bra wouldn't consider hers, greying with elastic worms coming out of the straps. They can probably be up-cycled into something, lampshades or Christmas decorations, she can almost imagine them in the craft gallery and she has been known to use old holey knickers as floorcloths but there's less to a bra, less absorbency. It's not much colder outside than in, Matt's right, they will have to put the heating on, next cold snap, they don't need any more mould in the bathroom, but these clouds have been around all night and yesterday, insulating things, it's pretty good for the time of year. Well, not good, obviously, it should be colder than this, bad but convenient. She leaves the door open and wanders down the garden. There will be daffodils along the path here in spring, and tulips over there, the dark purple ones sold as black. She's never planted so many bulbs before. Good thing she bought them while she was still on full pay. The kale's holding up, they should have some more of that tonight though it feels as if all her cooking has turned into the same thing, some kind of vegetable and tinned tomato slop on rice, grated cheese if you're desperate. They need to eat less dairy, there's no real excuse not to be vegan but Matt wouldn't have it and she hasn't tried all that hard, because of cheese, mostly, and because they eat so many beans already. She hadn't realised how much she relied on what came from the café, quiches and whatever salads wouldn't last another day, there was a scheme to deliver some of the leftovers to people living on the streets but the van came only twice a week and the other days the staff divvied it up, squabbling over Jo's lentil thing with the horseradish and being polite about the coleslaw. God knows what the homeless people are eating now though from what she's heard provision's been a bit better since the pandemic, turns out when people are worried about catching something from street sleepers there's suddenly funding available for safe places to stay and hot meals. Kate sees a slug, silvery on the pine-blue kale, pulls it off and puts it down on the bird table, wipes her hand on her jeans. She wishes sometimes you could just sign a disclaimer, like a Do Not Resuscitate order, promising that if you get sick you won't go to hospital, won't make any demands or expect any help, and in exchange you could take your own risks, decide how much you want to stay alive and at what cost to your sanity, but of course that's not how it works, it's not that the government care if you feel ill or die cheaply at home, it's that they care if you pass the illness to people who will die expensively in hospital so it's no use individuals trying to opt out, we're biologically connected to each other and anyway that's not how society works, she knows that, you can't sign out of community and it's not that she'd usually want to. She doesn't disapprove of lockdown or masks or any of it, not on principle, only the longer this goes on the less she objects to dying and the harder it is to understand why other people don't feel the same way.

There's birdsong now, some small piping voice in the hedge; wind, not much, in the bare apple tree. From here she can see across the fields to the hill, where the bracken is dying and the heather dull brown, cloud brushing the summit. It feels like another country, up there, especially in winter when there's no one around, when you can walk an hour or two before you see someone else, you and the wind and the sky. She can see from here there's no one on the path, she'd actually be further from another soul there, less likely to pass on disease, than she is here not two metres from Alice's garden not to mention the Amins on the other side and Samira in and out of old folks' homes, so worried she wouldn't come over even in the summer, I'd love to Kate, you know I would, but with you working in the café, it's too much risk, I'd never forgive myself if I gave it to a client. It will be quiet up there, the cloud muffling sound rising from the valley, and if you go far enough over the tops you come to places where you can't hear traffic. There used to be planes, you used to be able to watch them circling Manchester airport, banking and winging west to America and south to Europe, but now there are only birds in the sky. There'll be wind through the sleeping winter heather, and the bracken bright brown and the streams running cold and clear, the grass in the bogs grey now and lying long in the pools and no scent on the wind, just winter, everything biding its time, gathering strength underground, sleeping and waiting for the darkest days, the hinge of the year and then the return of the light; leaves gone and branches bare but the roots still working their way through the earth, the sheep huddled in their wool but pregnant, earth sodden and swollen with autumn's rainfall. Kate's back in the house changing the wellies for hiking boots, taking the backpack she keeps packed for hillwalking from under the coats on the hook, filling a water bottle and grabbing a packet of biscuits, and she's out of the front door, fast up the path, through the gate and out onto the lane. She pulls her hat and gloves from her coat pockets, puts them on as she walks. She couldn't come within spitting distance of another person if she wanted to, out here, and she won't be long, just an hour before sunset, she'll be back before Matt even knows she's gone.

watching the badgers

MATT'S FINISHED HIS Maths and he's hungry. The house is still unlit and silent, but on the landing he calls, Mum? Mum, you here? Her bedroom door is open, the way he left it, and even in the darkness he can see that there's no one there. Although usually he wouldn't bother, can move around this house just fine at night, he turns on the light to go down the stairs and sees her wellies lying in the hall. He doesn't think they were there earlier, so maybe she was out and has come in, come in very quietly and without turning on a light. The kitchen is also dark, but he goes in to see if she might be in the bathroom. There's no light under the door. She isn't in the front room either. He goes back to the hall, pushes his big feet into her small wellies and minces to the back door, which is unlocked. The cat appears and peers out, decides sensibly against it. It's fully dark now, no moon, only the shadow of the house blocked out by the street light at the front. He can still see the apple tree, many-fingered against the sky, and the stones of the flagged path. Mum, he calls, Mum? If she's fallen, maybe? Mum! He'd be able to see her, if she were lying here, and how could she fall, raking leaves? Mum! He turns back, excites the cat by going into the kitchen and opening the cupboard where they keep cat food as well as the first-aid kit, the box of batteries, candles for power cuts and a torch. The torch needs new batteries but it'll do for now, and he goes back out and blunders around on the wet grass, making sure.

Back in the house he tugs off her little boots. OK, fine, she's gone out when she shouldn't have done. It's not exactly surprising but she could have told him. If you're going up the hills, she's been saying to him probably since he could walk, don't go alone and if you do go alone tell someone where you're going and when you plan to be back, not that he does go up the hills much. Summer, sometimes, with friends, picnic and mucking about at the waterfall. So what's she playing at? Maybe she hasn't gone up the hills, maybe just to the woods or up the lane. He's going to call her. He hears over the burr of his phone the tinkle of hers, the old-fashioned jingle he gave up trying to make her change. This is Kate, please leave— He ends the call and tries again, this is Kate, please— tracks her ringtone up the stairs and then doesn't need the sound to find her phone plugged in by her bed, where it's probably been all day and maybe longer. Right then. OK. We have conclusively established, he thinks, that Mum has left the

house, has broken quarantine, and is out somewhere without her phone. Mum has broken the law. So there you go.
He'll just have to wait, and meanwhile he might as well
cook, have something ready for her when she comes back.

He feeds the cat. The sound of the biscuits falling into
the bowl seems to echo off the kitchen walls.

He does cook proper dinners sometimes. Well, once or
twice. He opens the fridge, which is half-empty. Eggs,
from the farm up the road, either been there over a week
or Mum went out another time and he doesn't think she
did. Need eating, then. Omelette, he can do that and not
much washing up either, though he'll have to wash the
frying pan before he gets started. No cheese, what else can
you put in an omelette? He looks it up on his phone: Spanish omelette, which requires you to have cooked potatoes
already; ham, nope; mushrooms, maybe? He opens the
drawers at the bottom of the fridge, which are usually the
last staging post before the compost heap. There are some
grey wrinkled things like long-dead slugs which he remembers being parsnips once. There's a brown paper bag but
it contains something that looks like miniature ginger root
and is orange inside when he snaps it. He sniffs it, good,
can still smell, and not ginger. And not mushrooms.
Smoked salmon, suggests the internet, fresh herbs. How
about kale, he wonders, could that play the role of a fresh
herb? Not that he wants to go out there and contend with
the real slugs. Masala omelette, which wants onion, green

chilli and a bunch of spices that are probably in the cupboard. That'll do. And the pan doesn't need to be all that clean, cheese toasties and omelettes are close enough.

He peels an onion, starts chopping. He's cold. Put another jumper on, she'd say. He can't remember Mum ever breaking the law before. Not speeding, the car doesn't go all that fast anyway, you'd worry something would fall off. There's a roll of duct tape in the glove compartment for good reasons, but she wouldn't drive fast even in a better car, doesn't really like driving at all because of the risk of hurting someone. Probably the nearest he's come to dying is last year when she skidded on the hill doing an emergency stop to avoid a rabbit. I'd never forgive myself, she says, if I hurt someone, but he's thinking that he's not sure she ever forgives herself anyway. For being alive, for having a carbon footprint, for using the NHS, not that she does use it, much. Most things get better if you wait, she says, we'll leave the doctor for people who need her. What if she does need a doctor, what if she's fallen out there, in the dark? He tips the onions into the pan, wipes his nose on the back of his hand. That's onions, not emotion. She doesn't fall, her night vision is better than his, she's just watching the badgers. Or whatever. He finds the jug and cracks eggs, should possibly have washed them first because there's chicken poo and bits of straw on the shell. Checks his phone with an eggy finger, you're supposed to add the chopped chilli and spices to the egg, chilli flakes will have to do. The cat comes and winds around his ankles and he bends to pet her. Where's Mum got to then, he asks her. Did you see her go, you daft thing?

The spices are all in little glass jars, unlabelled. He opens something that looks like cumin, sniffs, right sort of sweaty smell, gets a nose of chilli from what's clearly not paprika. His eyes stream, he can't really smell the next one but chucks some in anyway and the onions are a bit burnt. He picks out some of the black bits. She's not going to be back, is she, in time to eat this? He beats up the eggs, pushes the onion into the jug so he can cook half the mixture now and save half, which is also a reason not to wash the pan again. More oil, stop it sticking, and half the egg back in, OK a generous half but he always eats more than Mum does. He looks out, into the garden, suddenly doesn't like seeing himself and the kitchen reflected out there, the toaster and kettle under the skeletal tree, the fruit bowl with its never-ripening pears on the dewy grass. He folds the omelette, not bad, and squashes it a bit so the uncooked egg runs out. No one'd post a photo but it looks edible, and on second thoughts he does post a photo.

Doesn't take long to eat a small omelette. He squeezes a pear, but they're still not ripe. There might be a bit of ice cream left but he's too cold. The biscuit tin is empty and the packet he thought he'd seen in the cupboard isn't there. Toast and jam, then. He takes a new loaf from the freezer, not looking at his reflection in the window, and uses the bread knife to lever slices off the end. And tea, Mum'll be glad to find tea in the pot when she comes in.

He takes his toast back upstairs, gets under the duvet, flicks around for something to watch but there isn't anything he fancies and he doesn't feel like going back to the game. The cat comes to curl up on his belly. He maybe dozes a little.

receding mirrors and people lost

ALICE IS HAVING dinner with Susie and John. She keeps a pile of cookbooks on the kitchen table now, so she can stand the iPad at an angle that means her double chin doesn't put her off her food, and a bedside lamp with a warm-toned bulb so she doesn't look dead. They'll get a shock if they ever see her for real again, fatter and paler and more wrinkled than she is on screen. Things have gone south, these last months, further and faster south. Though maybe the same will turn out to be true of Susie, she's coming to that age, hard to tell on the screen because with all of them there everyone's further away and always moving about; Susie never did really insist that the children sat at the table and now half the time they have their phones by their plates, their screens on her screen, receding mirrors and people lost in them.

Susie leans in to the screen, as if she'd be able to see into more of Alice's house from a different angle, as if the iPad were a window. What have you got there, Mum, did you cook yourself something nice? Alice pokes at her plate. No, she baked cookies instead. Just a supermarket chicken curry, she says, they can be surprisingly good but I have to say this one isn't. It'll do. You need to eat properly, Mum, Susie says, fruit and veg, you won't rebuild your immune system on cookies, are you sure you don't want me to order online shopping for you? Quite sure, thank you darling, Alice says. I was using the internet before you were born, she wants to say, which isn't true, obviously, but she was using computers before it was easy, when you still had to type command lines and more or less do your own programming as you went along. The Extreme Vulnerability, she wants to say, is about my cancer, not my IT skills. Susie forks something into her mouth from below the camera and talks through it. *I* have to say, she says, I sometimes think when this is over I'm never cooking again, it's going to be bread and cheese or takeaway for years. But Mum, you won't ever get a takeaway, says Seb from off-screen, we wanted pizza tonight and you wouldn't. Too expensive, Susie says, no change out of fifty quid with the four of us and a tip, we can eat for days on that. How's work? asks Alice, a carefully neutral question because last time she talked to Susie without John, Susie said it was looking as if John might lose his job and if that happens, as far as Alice can see, they're stuffed, there's no way they can live on Susie's salary. She'd help, she supposes, well, obviously, rather than see them lose the house, though that silly car was always an extravagance and they say it's her generation destroying the environment not to mention pillaging the welfare state and generally leaving nothing for anyone else, as if none of them care about their grand-children. Of course she'd help, but they've given Susie a lot over the years, some serious sums, and it doesn't actually seem to improve her life, not in the long term, and it's probably Alice's fault, Susie's haplessness, feck-lessness even, she must have failed to teach her and maybe it would be better, or would have been better, not to help, it's not as if anyone came along and gave her and Mark ten grand when they needed a car and fifty for a house, they saved up and worked it out but then that first house cost what, three times Mark's salary of the day, not that they didn't do a lot of work on it, by which she means with their own four hands, evenings and weekends, learning to tile a floor and plumb a sink, her hair, long then, in a shower cap for painting a ceiling. It cemented the marriage, she's some-times thought, all those late nights being the two persons on a two-person job, buggering things up and sorting them out together. She's not sure Susie can even change a tyre but then whose fault is that, it's not as if there's a statute of limitation on blaming your mum.

Oh, says Susie, we're OK, same old, you know. What have you been up to? Same old, Alice wants to say, two can play at that game and the best news anyone has these days is that nothing much has changed, but she says I've done some baking, I put on that 70s playlist you made for me, Seb, and had a good old dance around the kitchen, got out into the garden a bit this morning, planted the last of the bulbs, and we've a good book coming up in the book group, you might like it. I've no time for reading, Susie says, it's all very well people on furlough going on about reading and yoga and baking, I've been working all hours. I'm not on furlough, Alice wants to say, I'm retired, remember, and I did my time at work, all those years, doing my bit, and you'd rather I was reading than moping, wouldn't you? You do sound busy, she says, I hope you're taking some time to yourself, are you getting out for a walk? No, says Susie, I told you, Claire wants us all online eight-thirty to five-thirty, she gets snarky if she thinks someone's gone off to pee or make a cup of tea, and then it's dark out and the kids wanting their dinner and the house a tip with all of us home all the time and where would I go, anyway?

Sometimes Alice thinks she'd rather have a Radio 4 podcast than Susie with her dinner.

And how are you, Seb, she asks. How's school? And where's Laura this evening? It seems unbelievable to her that the schools are open again, children taking

buses and the Tube, sitting in classrooms, eating together, good for them of course, but you wonder about
the poor teachers, Sheila worried sick Amber's going to
fall ill but apparently Amber says she'd risk the classroom any day rather than be stuck at home trying to
teach Chemistry to teenagers on their phones. Alice
did, at least, send Seb and Laura a laptop each – basic,
reconditioned – the week the schools closed and then,
guilty, donated rather less than the cost of a laptop to
the village school, but it's something, isn't it, she can't
buy laptops for every child in England, wouldn't it be
unnatural not to save your own when you can? Seb
appears briefly, dizzyingly, so close to the camera that
half his nose and one eye fill the screen. School-y, he
says. My teacher's off for two weeks and they've sent
a horrible woman instead. I'm sorry about that, Alice
says, why is she horrible? He appears again, mouth
full, chewing. Strict, he says, and she hates the boys,
teachers always hate the boys, it's sexism. He's gone. Is
your teacher in quarantine? she asks. Not that there
would be much risk to Seb, really, from what Alice can
work out it would actually be better for kids to catch
it while they're young, like chicken pox, but Susie
and John are old enough to worry and neither of them
exactly slim or fit, they drink too much, is Alice's opinion, bottle of wine every night as far as she can tell
and John often taking a whisky nightcap, spending a

lot on your drink doesn't make it any better for you. Dunno, says Seb, probably, Shamshere's quarantining, and Ruben and lots of the girls. So's my neighbour, Alice says, you know Kate and Matt next door, it's going round Matt's school and there was a case at Kate's café, while they were still open for takeaway. Susie puts her glass down. But they get your shopping for you, don't they? I hope you haven't been too close, you've been wiping the groceries the way we told you, haven't you? I've been wiping things, Alice wants to say, since before you were born, and a whole lot more after you were born, don't tell the person who changed your nappies how to wipe things. I've been being very careful, she says, I don't want to catch it any more than you do.

Her curry has gone cold, which doesn't really matter, it wasn't nice enough to be worth the calories anyway and the rice is inexcusable; the cookies might be fattening but at least they taste good. She'll have an orange first, once this call is over. An orange and a bowl of cookies and ice cream, on a tray in front of the television, and a cup of that sugar-free hot chocolate, and then up to bed with the electric blanket and her book, and tomorrow she'll cook properly, with vegetables.

Though I saw her, Kate, she says, going out, off for a walk I think, I suppose she couldn't take it any more and I can't say I blame her, what harm can it do for her to go up the hill a bit on her own? Wait, says Susie,

what? Are you telling us that Kate's supposed to be
self-isolating and you saw her leaving her house? Oh
hell, Alice thinks. Oh, she was probably just going up
the path, she says, certainly not out to meet anyone,
Kate wouldn't do that, she maybe just needed a turn
along the lane. But she's not allowed a turn along the
lane, Susie says. She's put her cutlery down. You should
call the police, Mum, she's breaking the law, there are
big fines, ten grand now, that's how serious it is, there's
a special hotline you can call. I'm not calling the police
on Kate, Alice says. What, for going out for a little walk
on her own, up the lane here, when she's not even sick?
She couldn't afford a fine, you know that, single mum,
laid off from the café. She'll be on furlough from the
café now, Susie says, they've closed all the cafés near
you, Mum, you know that. She'll be getting paid for
doing nothing and all she has to do is park her backside
on her sofa and stay there, it's not exactly slave labour.
Not everyone, Alice thinks, finds it as easy to park
their backside on a sofa and stay there as Susie does.
She sees the need for quarantine, she does, she's not
some raving conspiracy theorist, but to call the police
because an innocent woman's gone for a walk— She'll
be getting paid less than when she was working, Alice
says, and I very much doubt she was ever doing better
than breaking even on full pay with tips, but that's not
the point, Suze, it's not about money, she's not doing

any harm and anyway I'm not calling the police on my neighbours, not until I see them burying bodies in the back garden. Someone will be burying bodies, Susie says, if infected people keep wandering around in public, that's why they make the laws, Mum. She was just a close contact, Alice says, we don't know if she's infected or not, I'm sure she wouldn't have gone out if she had symptoms. I'll call her later, talk to her about it. You know they've been very kind. Yes, well, says Susie, she's not being very kind now, it's not very kind to go out and transmit a fatal disease, tramping about for fun while other people are stuck behind a computer screen working to pay their taxes so some people can have weeks and weeks off. No, love, Alice says, it's not, I'll talk to her. Only on the phone, says Susie, don't you go round there. I still think you should call the police. John, don't you think we should call the police? Tell me her surname and I'll do it myself. She's gone for a walk on her own, Alice says again, up a country lane in November. She's been shut up for days. She's not gone to dance at a party or sweat all over a gym. The whole village will be onto it if anyone calls the police, we've already had some of that in the first lockdown and it wasn't pretty. Of course I won't call round there, I haven't set foot outside the gate in weeks, I'm not going to mess it all up tonight. Now then, where's Laura this evening? Bedroom, Susie says, she won't come down and I've run out of energy to make her do it, she can get herself a sandwich later. Or not, I'm past caring, she won't waste away. Poor Laura, Alice has the sense not to say. She'll text her granddaughter later, see if they can have a private chat.

remember o thou man

KATE IS OUT and moving, going somewhere, the hill rising under her feet and the sky ahead of her. Wind in the trees and her body working at last, climbing, muscle and bone doing what they're made for. She won't be long, really she won't, only a sip of outside, fast up the lane and over the fields, just a little way up the stone path for a quick greeting to the fells. She'll come near no one; there won't be hikers out here now, barely an hour of daylight left, nothing in the weather to call folk onto the hills. There's only Breck End up the lane and she won't even follow the path up the side of the farmyard, she'll walk wide over the field, not chat to Jill's horses the way she usually does, because if mink can catch it from people, why not horses, don't they say the first common cold came from a horse but this one goes the other way, cats and dogs catching it from their owners. Colour is fading from the moor ahead, but the chestnut tree by the wall is full of starlings in loud conversation and the bumps of next year's buds already swelling on the branches. Normally she'd pause to admire the starlings — so pretty, their speckles and their iridescence — but she's not wasting this stolen time pausing, there's plenty of pausing going on indoors all over Europe. She strides on, feels the grip of boots on tarmac, the dullness of wet leaves. There's grass down the middle of this road, still poking green through the mud, and brimming potholes reflecting the bare branches overhead. Damp, not quite raining. Keep moving, get warm. The relief of it, being out, being alone, starting to warm up from her own effort, wind and sky in her lungs, raindrops on her face, weather. There'll be a scarf and extra mittens in the backpack, probably, she usually keeps them there, it's always easier to get out of the door if the bag's already packed, but best save them for the higher ground, good to have something else to put on above the treeline. The beat of her feet, the beat of her heart, pick up.

The lights are on already at Breck End, and from the track she can see Jill moving around the kitchen, one of the kids blue in the light of a screen upstairs. Off school again, must be. And there's Neil going into the barn, Kate's about to call and wave when she remembers, presses herself instead into the deepening shadow of the hedge. It's like skiving school, she thinks, the way they used to try to sneak down the drive to the shops for sweets and crisps, crouching and dashing from bush to bush. She's an outlaw. She pulls her hood forward over her face, waits until Neil's gone to climb the stile. Will Jill recognise her if she looks up and sees someone crossing the field? Best just go fast, not that Jill would – but you can't tell, any more, who will understand, it's surprising who turns out to think going outside at all is unnecessary and it's ridiculous, everyone knows indoor transmission is the problem, if the people in charge had any sense they'd be setting limits on how many hours you can spend inside, shooing people out into the wind and the fresh air instead of locking us in. When did we become a species whose default state is shut up indoors? Earlier for women than men, probably, men always setting things up to have the best bits themselves, though Matt would say war and street violence and he's not wrong, the girls are walking the boys home these days, less likely to get stabbed with girls around. Were walking the boys home. When they went out in the first place. Has knife crime dropped, and if so, by more than domestic violence has risen? We're a living experiment, she thinks, in the intensive farming of humans, which is another silly overstatement, no one's force-feeding us antibiotics or cutting bits off us so we can't run away and it's all the name of safety, not profit. Well, mostly, give or take— Whisht, whisht. Look at the sheep, safely grazing. Look at the dry-stone walls, some of which probably stood through the Spanish Flu and even the Black Death. Look at the oak, twisted and bony, the last tree before she crosses the stone footbridge and the moor rises up under the sky. Listen to the wind over the heather.

Dusk is slow this time of year. She still has a little while. She should make it at least up to the col, to where the old stone packhorse route crosses the hill and you can see across the high plateau towards the city below. She's seen photos of the city now, quiet on a weekday lunchtime as it used to be – well, never, really, not since they ended the Sunday closing. There's no point in thinking about how this will ever end. All the other plagues ended, sooner or later, though most of them went away as well as coming back, some years, some decades, better than others, and people lived and loved and built houses and planted trees and made food and clothes and – and stained glass, travelled, even, made music and put on plays. Ring a ring o' roses. Smallpox, typhoid, cholera: probably more people have lived through epidemics than not over the last few centuries. And of course life won't go back to the way it was, it never does and rarely should. There will be holes in the children's education, a generation that's forgotten or never learnt how to go to a party, people of all ages who won't forget to be afraid to leave the house, to be afraid of other people, afraid to touch or dance or sing, to travel, to try on clothes – whisht, she thinks again, hush now. Walk. The bracken has died back, its copper turned to bronze, and the bare heather stands delicate as frost. Cloud hangs low; there's something satisfying about a properly grey English day, about the back end of a winter afternoon with no pretensions of sunset. Remember o thou man, she sings, o thou man, o thou man. She stopped singing, even in the shower, weeks ago, it only reminded her— Remember o thou man, thy time is spent. She's always loved those fabulously gloomy carols, sorrowing sighing bleeding dying, sealed in a stone-cold tomb. From depths of Hell thy people save, and give them victory o'er the grave. She takes a breath, slows her steps to a procession (down the aisle, candle in hand, robes swaying in the draught). Remember o thou man, how thou art dead and gone, and I did what I can, therefore repent. She holds a high D, harmonising against the unsung melody, takes a proper breath and becomes an alto, skipping the next verse where it's a pig trying to match the words to the music, she doesn't want to sing about God's goodness anyway. The angels all did sing, o thou man, o thou man, the angels all did sing, upon the shepherds' hill. Sing out to the sky, to the city on the plain. The angels all did sing, praise to our heavenly king. There will be no singing in the churches this year, in the schools and pubs, so we should sing on the mountain, while we're compelling people to do and not do all sorts of ridiculous things we should mandate singing on mountains. More exaggeration, it's not a mountain, barely two-thirds of a mountain by the generally accepted definition. Hush, sing. To Bethlem did they go, o thou man, o thou man, and as she comes to the end, to be not afraid, there's another voice, low words on the hill above. Not the first time she's been caught singing and walking, embarrassed Matt a few times when he would still come with her though when he was little she used to coax him over the moor with silly variations on the coming round the mountain song. She'll be eating purple pansies when she comes, she'll be fleeing smelly lizards when she comes. Oh but she's not supposed to be here, better turn off the path right now though there have been days, many days these last months, when those walkers' greetings – ayup, lovely day for it, morning, all right love – are the best thing that happens, the moment she remembers later when she can't sleep and she's looking for reasons to stay alive till morning, the casual goodwill of strangers still, despite – the voice speaks again and she sees that there's no one on the path, that it's coming from a raven on a rock ahead. The raven looks at her and calls, unharmonious, possibly heckling. Fine then. She takes a lungful of winter air, starts again, louder, the angels all did sing, o thou man, o thou man. O thou bird. You couldn't say ravens sing, but she (she?) is certainly participating. Alto, tenor, reed, woodwind, but actually just a different sound entirely, bird music. Kate listens, sings back something near the raven's call, waits for the response, sings a third higher, again, back down, a quick arpeggio, gets a reply that sounds like laughter. I should go, raven, she sings, dark is falling. Benighted, she thinks, thus threading dark-eyed night, where's that from? She sings the line to the raven, who doesn't know. Just a little further, then, a little longer, no one could expect her to resist evensong with a raven.

The raven goes with her up the stone path, flying ahead, landing on a rock, waiting for Kate to catch up, fluttering on. Ravens do this, she remembers, this isn't a personal encounter, the bird has no message for her, they're just clever and curious and not particularly scared of people. The moor is dim now, fading into the sky, but the flagstones under her feet lead clear across the tops and when she looks back the lights of Breck End are bright. Once she's there she can find her way home down the lane no matter the night. Should be her headtorch in the backpack, push come to shove, not that she'll be long enough to need it. The wind lifts her hair and she takes in a deep breath of winter moorland, peat and rainwater. The bulk of the hill ahead stands against the cloud, and below the orange lights of the village begin to glow. The raven calls her to hurry up, nearly there, just for a glimpse of the tops, just to promise her return. There. Kate reaches the packhorse track, worn deep between its stone walls; further on it becomes the coffin path, used before the roads came to bear the dead from high farms and hamlets abandoned now, down to the churches in the valley. She walks along it, fast on the smoother path, just to the point where the Grindsbrook route branches off towards the Woolpacks (no sense in carrying a coffin through the rock formations; all the old paths take the easiest routes). The main trail swings north: Swine's Back, Edale Rocks, Kinder Low, the edge route to the Downfall and then the great northern march over Alport, Black Ashop Moor and Bleaklow, on, if you like, over Bare Holme Moss, Black Hill, Saddleworth, along England's backbone into Yorkshire, Cumbria, the Borders. She murmurs the names to herself but she's not going much further now, she's really not, though from only a mile or two the great rocks call her through the fading light. Pym's Chair, the Woolpacks. They're easy to climb, mostly, from behind, and then you can sit on the edge with your feet dangling over open air, sip tea from your flask and watch the weather pass until you feel almost airborne, part of the sky.

The raven sits on the Public Footpath sign, waiting. Kate climbs the stile but only for a vantage point, only to see out. Matt will be wanting dinner. She looks over the rolling moor where night is settling, towards the Tower. Not now, she shouldn't have stayed so long. Well, of course she shouldn't be here at all, maybe they were right at school that breaking one rule makes it logical to break another until the commandments fall like dominos, the saved and damned forever divided by the colour of their socks, uniform violations the gateway to murder and theft. Not that it wouldn't be a public service to murder some people, if she had to make a list there are names that come to mind. Though it's easy enough to murder people in your head, what Matt never realised is that the real reason she did the emergency stop for the rabbit that time wasn't that she was afraid of killing it but that she was afraid of not killing it, of maiming or mutilating, because she knows she could not look a suffering creature in the eye and end its misery as it should be ended, because she would have been shuddering and probably puking there on the road, unable to finish the job. It's not always a sign of character, the desire to rescue drowning insects. Sometimes it would be better to hurt a fly. The raven calls her back to the job in hand, which is to get off the mountain while she can still, more or less, see her feet, but the voice comes from just a little further up, from the faint path to the rolling high ground where there's no summit, exactly, just a great expanse of moorland under the sky where you can walk for hours using the rocks and lonely rowan trees for landmarks. It's like walking on water, she sometimes thinks, like walking over ocean swell, and the wind ruffling the heather and the bog cotton the way it ruffles the sea, and like the sea the dangers are at the edges, where water and rock drop to the valleys. Just a little further, then, another raven-flight into the dusk, because it's irresistible, because she feels at home up here in the dark now, in the friendly presence of stones and sheep after all those days locked up in the house, all those nights waking at 3 am and lying there trying to remember that in the morning, or one day in the future in which she does not believe, she will be glad that she didn't walk out over the fields to the railway line, because it wouldn't be so bad for the driver, would it, in the dark, he wouldn't have to see much of her because the trains come pretty fast across the hillside and there are two places where a footpath crosses the line and it's not even lit, just signs telling you to be careful and that there are fines for trespassing on the railway but not, presumably, if you're dead. You could turn your back to the train, save the driver seeing your face, though of course you'd rather see it coming, stare into its lights. Not that there are so many trains, not since last year, now no one goes anywhere, but the point is Matt, isn't it, not the train timetable, the point is that single parents should stay alive if only to earn the money, not that she's earning enough money, and if walking a few more minutes, another mile or so, over the darkening hill makes it easier to stay alive, what harm does it do?

ringing from the other room

MATT GETS UP, stiff in the cold, puts the cat back in the warm patch. You can tell when a house is empty. He stands on the landing, the way he used to do when he was little and wanted to hear the grown-ups downstairs, catch the background music of whatever Dad was watching or hear Mum on the phone, not the words but just the sounds, the light coming from the front room and the blue flicker of the television. There's silence, darkness, and she doesn't stay out this long, she's not raking leaves or watching badgers. Mum's gone.

He doesn't know what to do.

He goes down the stairs, and then back up, back to his room where he turns the light on and sits on the bed, beside the cat. He strokes her and then stands up to look out of the window. Mum might even now be coming down the lane, about to open the gate, but there's no one under the streetlight, just a soft rain and the trees black against the dark. Alice's light is on. He goes back to the bed, picks up his phone to try Mum, as if she might some-how have come back and taken her phone and gone out again, but he doesn't want to hear it ringing from the other room. He strokes the cat, who shakes her head against his hand and tucks her nose back into her folded legs. She wants to sleep.

He doesn't know what to do. Normally you call the police when someone's gone missing, don't you, but he doesn't know if that would be 999, it doesn't seem like an emergency, exactly, or that other number, and he does know that at least on TV they won't do anything when the person is an adult with every right to leave home and go somewhere else, not for at least forty-eight hours, but Kate doesn't have the right to leave home or go anywhere and there's a big fine for breaking quarantine, he can't remem-ber how much but whatever it is they can't afford it and anyway he doesn't want Mum to be arrested, he just wants her back, or at least wants to know where she is. That would do, it's not that he can't cope on his own, it's not that he's never gone to bed alone in the house or that he can't feed himself and the cat and hang the laundry and put the bins out — if they're allowed to put the bins out, he can't remember, would there be a worry about the bin men touching something he's touched — it's not that, if she wants to be somewhere else, if she's star-gazing or something that's fine, but she didn't say she was going out, he doesn't even know when she went, and people don't do that, just disappear, do they, he always tells her when he's going out even if he might sometimes have been a little vague about where, back when you could go places, when the King's Head was open and not looking too hard at your ID on a Saturday night as long as you behaved yourself. He never just disappeared on her. He might not always have answered his phone, hasn't always been the best at charging it, but he's always had it with him. That's what you do, isn't it, that's what people do, you don't just walk out on your family.

He strokes the cat again. She ignores him.

He doesn't know what to do.

her electric blanket

ALICE DRAWS THE curtains, folds up the bedspread, sets it at the foot of the bed, moves the silk cushions to the chair. She turns on the electric blanket, a moment she anticipates all day. It's not that she keeps the house cold, it's properly insulated and she's too old and too well-off for that nonsense, but there's something about a heated bed, about the luxury of stretching out your chilly feet into tender warmth and knowing that you can stay where you are for hours, that's better than pretty much anything. It's a hug, a warm embrace, except that you can read in it, leave it on all night or turn it off any time you like. She sometimes thinks an electric blanket is better than sharing a bed, doesn't snore or fart or hog the duvet, which is almost certainly not true as well as being disloyal and unkind and Mark would never have dreamt of saying such a thing, but then she's not saying it, is she, she wouldn't say it. It's just that it turns out that Pat and Kathleen were wrong when they told her that going to bed on your own is the loneliest point of the widow's day, that's all. Cooking dinner, for example, is pretty lonely, Mark used to pour her a glass of wine and potter about emptying the dishwasher and chatting and getting in her way while she chopped and stirred. Enough of that. She should probably have a shower, it's been a day or two, but – well not tonight, who wants to stand about in a shower when you could just go to bed with another day done and the second half of your book to carry you into the night? She will, though, brush her teeth, hasn't fallen that far, especially after all today's sugar, God knows when she'll be able to see a dentist again. She must remember to ask for a new toothbrush this week, very sweet of Kate to buy that bamboo one but the shape is all wrong, very old-fashioned, there must be some reason why biodegradable toothbrushes can't be properly shaped and at her age she's sorry but not setting off her gums again is a higher priority than saving a teaspoonful of plastic, it's not as if one toothbrush is going to break the camel's back, they should make supermarkets stop packaging everything the way they do before coming for an old lady's toothbrush.

She's squeezing toothpaste when the doorbell rings, a short, tentative buzz, and she's already taken off her glasses and watch. I'm not answering the door, she thinks, this time of night, who do they take me for. She hasn't even had to think about locking up, the front door's been double-locked for days, no reason to open it. Who on earth is going round ringing people's bells at this hour? Though you'd expect someone like that, someone intending to insist, to press longer. She waits for it to come again, waits another minute, and then goes through to the bedroom, toothbrush in hand, can't see her glasses on the bedside table, finds them, pushes back a corner of the curtain and peers round and there's Matt, walking away down the garden path, all hunched and not wearing a coat. He shouldn't be out either, certainly shouldn't be coming round here, what are they playing at today, Matt and Kate? Of course she's not going to call the police, but really— She sees Matt's face under the streetlamp. He's wearing a mask and she can't see properly, but something in his walk, in the way he's holding himself— Alice opens the curtain, pushes the sash window up. Matt! Is something wrong?

He turns back, rain on his hair. She remembers him little, splashing in puddles in an all-in-one rain suit with ridiculous yellow ducks on it, why do they design things like that when ducks aren't yellow? He comes up the path. He shouts, she can't hear. I can't hear you, she calls, take off that mask, you're not going to infect anyone standing there. He pulls it down. Don't come down, he shouts, you mustn't come near me, I put my hand in a bag to ring the bell, see and then I stood right back. He does indeed have a plastic bag on his hand. Yes, she says, never mind all that, what's wrong? He pauses, there in the rain, looks down. Matt, she says, what is it? Nothing, he says, sorry, I shouldn't have bothered you, it was a mistake, I'm really sorry, I shouldn't have left the house. You won't tell anyone, will you? I didn't touch anything, I used the bag to open both gates. It's not bloody leprosy, she says, you're not unclean, what's wrong? He's backing away. Nothing, he says, it's all right, I'm sorry, good night. Matt, she yells, if you don't come back here and tell me what the problem is I'm going to come out there after you right now in my pyjamas and catch my death of cold, never mind anything else.

He turns back. Sorry, he shouts, I don't know what to do. This is ridiculous, she thinks, I can't help the lad like this. Stay there, she says, I'm going to come down and put a mask on and you stand in the porch and I'll stand in the hall and you can tell me about it, we're not shouting at each other. You're not ill, are you? No, he says, I'm not ill, neither of us has been ill, but don't do that, really— She shuts the window, puts her cardigan back on over the pyjamas, fluffy slippers, give the lad a laugh if nothing else. Down the stairs almost too fast, when did she last hurry anywhere, coat not worn probably since last year and where's a mask, Susie sent her a dozen which was a bit daft since the whole point is that she doesn't go anywhere, doesn't see anyone. Pulls her ears, doesn't work with glasses, no wonder people hate them. Where's the front door key? Where are some shoes? You're still there, she calls, aren't you? Don't go away, Matt. It's your mum, isn't it? It's Kate.

the fragile stem

pain

cold

wind

noise

breathing hurts

The noise is a voice.
Her voice.
Stop it, that won't help, what's the point of that?
Quiet. Rainfall, wind. Rock leaning over her, dark against dark sky.

She's lying on the ground, in the heather. Running water. There's something on her face, the smell of sheep shit. Parasites, aren't there? The pain.

Kate breathes in slowly. Pain in her back and at the front in her ribs and she's not thinking about the leg. She turns her head, hears the rustle of her coat on the heather. It hurts.

She moves one hand and then the other. It hurts.

One foot works.

Don't think about the leg.

Cold.

She's not wearing the rucksack. She reaches for it, where it ought to be, as much as she can without turning. No. Did she take it off, up there? She doesn't remember, but don't think about that, remembering isn't what matters. She needs it, and the torch. Roll, she thinks, sit up, but her voice makes that noise again when she tries.

Don't think about the leg. Do think about the rucksack. There's shaking in her bones, cold, and the hair wet on her face.

Whatever else is wrong, she needs the rucksack because in the rucksack, unless she or Matt took them out sometime, there is a survival blanket and a first-aid kit.

Whatever else is wrong, getting colder will make things worse.

It crosses her mind that nothing in the little green first-aid kit is going to help.

It crosses her mind that – not now. Find the rucksack. Find the blanket.

She looks up through the heather. Rain in her eyes. One hand can reach out. Her back doesn't like it when the other arm moves. She feels around with the good hand, sweeps prickly heather and cold, slimy sheep shit. No. She's going to have to sit up. She tries again to roll towards the bad arm so the good one can push her up. Howls. Lies back. Shakes, ribs and shoulders shuddering against the earth.

This isn't going to work.

This has to work.

She counts a slow breath in, two three four, ow, out two three four.

Try again. Fine, howl. But try again.

The noise reminds her of childbirth, hearing sounds coming from herself.

The pain is worse.

Something that's probably the rucksack but possibly a stone is over there. Kate lies back. Right then. The first problem is the cold, because if she gets hypothermic she won't be able to address any of the other problems, and also because the cold is a problem with a solution and the solution is in the rucksack. If it is the rucksack. So she has to get the rucksack. The pain, she thinks, only feels more urgent than the cold. The pain probably won't get worse than it is now. But she will rest first, she will just lie here a moment in the rain.

No, she mustn't do that.

Her eyes want to close. She wants to sleep. The shaking is gentler than it was.

Matt. She left Matt.

Kate rolls, moans, pushes herself up. She can't hold this position. She tries to sit, but the leg—

Don't lie down again. Move towards the rucksack, one move. She leans on the good arm and tries to shuffle, whimpers. So whimper. Do it again.

You can't shuffle over heather. This isn't working.

This has to work. She left Matt. Crawl, then.

The leg— Drag the leg. Don't scream, breathe. In two three four, out two three four. There's some groaning.

Again. Stop at the rucksack, not before.

Again.

At least there's enough feeling in her hands for the heather to hurt. Kate grips it, feels splinters enter her palms. Good then, think of the small pain.

Wasn't she wearing gloves? Where are the gloves?

Again. A brief rest, just a moment, just a few breaths. Ow.

Her hood is slipping back. She tries to pull it up but the bad arm hurts too much and she needs the good one to hold her weight. Rain patters on her jacket. Don't think about the leg.

It is the rucksack. Thank the Lord for that. One more pull. One more, and she lowers herself to lie against the rucksack. Oh, her leg. It's the thigh, she allows herself to think, which isn't ideal because she remembers from first aid classes that the femur has a serious blood supply, one of those foolish bits of anatomical engineering though not as stupid as putting the brain and breathing apparatus wobbling about on the fragile stem of the neck. Kate lifts her good hand to her neck, to check the pulse, but the hand is too cold or she can't find the place or maybe she doesn't have a pulse, who cares, idle curiosity. She's alive, isn't she? She pushes herself up again, whimpers, bites her lip as she pushes at the rucksack with the bad hand because she needs the good one for leaning on. So this is going to be a long job, she thinks, which is OK because it will keep her busy, because once this job is done she will have to think about—

She's going to have to move either herself or the rucksack to reach the opening, rucksacks aren't designed to be opened with one hand, the clips and the drawstring. The shaking is starting again.

people who leave

YOU'RE GOING OUT, Ellie says, aren't you? You're doing it again. I have to, love, Rob says. There's someone out there, a lady lost on the hills. There's someone in here, Ellie says, there's your daughter here for her weekend with you, remember?

She follows him into the hall, where he's grabbing his coat, car keys, good thing he didn't change his muddy hiking trousers when he came in this afternoon. I'm really sorry, love, he says. I'll be back by morning, you know that, we'll have a great day together tomorrow, and Sunday. I'll make it up to you. You'd be going to bed soon anyway, wouldn't you, we're not missing much. You said, she says, you promised Mum you wouldn't be on the rota, access weekends. He's lacing his boots, looks up to see her leaning in the kitchen doorway, her hair gleaming under the light. She looks like her mum, he thinks, un-thinks. He wishes she wouldn't wear all that makeup and there's no need for it, is there, to hang out at home. I'm not on

83

the rota, he says, but we've three people in quarantine and two off sick and this is a big job, she was seen going onto the tops and she's left her phone at home, we've no idea where she might be. Also, he does not say, we worry about people who leave their phones, because it tends to mean they don't want to be found and as often as not by the time we do find them, they've done what they went up there for. And in this particular case, he does not say, there's a concern that the lady was maybe in a troubled state of mind, and also in this particular case there is a boy not much older than you, princess girl, who is now going to have to wait alone at home while we look for his mum, because he's not allowed to leave the house and no one else is allowed into it, and if, in the best remotely plausible scenario here, we do find her and take her to hospital, he won't be able to visit. So don't, princess girl, try to tell me that you are the one suffering most by this call-out. I'm really sorry, he says again, I'll let Beth and Nick know I'm going, you know you can pop next door if you need anything, or just call me. Look on the bright side, you get all the pizza and ice cream and you can watch whatever you like on the big screen while you eat it, sounds all right to me, no? No, she says, actually not, Dad, what sounds all right to me is you actually spending time with me, actually wanting to spend time with me in the two days we get, that's what sounds all right to me.

At least, his friend Fiona said, she can tell you how

she feels. At least she's not bottling things up. I know it won't feel like it but it's a really good sign, under it all you must have made a great relationship with her. There are times when he feels a little bottling up would be entirely acceptable.

I know, he says, I would much rather be with you, you must know I'd rather be on the sofa sharing the posh ice cream than crawling around on a mountain in the dark all night, but someone has to do it, sweetheart, there's a person lost and maybe injured out there, we can't just leave her, can we? You can just leave me, Ellie says. You're safe and well, he says, now you stay that way, OK? Beth and Nick, right, call me any time, don't do anything daft. I'll be back as soon as I can and tomorrow we'll do something amazing. Everything's closed, she says, no one's done anything amazing for months, you promise stuff you can't deliver just to get away from me. Goodnight, he says, take care of yourself. Yeah, well, no one else is going to, are they, she says, fine then. See you.

He listens to music on the way to the RV point. Loud music.

It's not exactly raining, but the road shines wet in the headlights and fine droplets settle on the windscreen as the road breasts the fell. Low cloud, mist, that kind of thing. Not ideal for the job in hand, but it's not cold, not for November. He remembers the woman last year, in the snow – and it's safe to pass the lorry here, nothing coming, gear change for the hill. Ellie will be all right, won't she, she's not cross enough to do something daft but that's the problem with teenagers, dodgy sense of proportion, volatile, she only needs to be in a silly frame of mind for as long as it takes to do some idiotic thing and then it's too late. If there's a minute spare he'll call her later, at least a text. All she has to do is stay home in the warm and eat ice cream, he's not exactly making unreasonable demands, is he? At her age he'd been working with his dad, evenings and weekends, a couple of years, no chance of anyone having that house to themselves ever except maybe sometimes Mum on a school day, working nights, nice to think she might have found a minute to herself. Rob turns up the gravel track to the quarry where they meet, sees the lights ahead of him. Everyone's out for this, full-scale job, all four MRTs, search dogs, they'll need the coastguard if chief wants a helicopter with visibility like this. He checks his phone as he gets out of the van. Nothing, which means that either Ellie's behaving herself or that the consequences of misbehaviour have not yet been discovered. She'll just have to cope. He hooks the mask around his ears, already clammy on his wet face.

The doors of the hut stand wide and the lights make it difficult to see his feet. It's hard to tell with everyone masked who's there: Lisa, spot the hair anywhere, and Craig, looks like. Miro, Johnson. Evening all, Rob says. Hi, Rob, how are you. Evening. He edges around them,

not that there's room for much distancing, grabs his kit
and stands out on the gravel beside Miro to pull on the
trousers, fasten the jacket, re-lace his boots. The rain picks
up, pattering on the waterproofs. Johnson tells them but
they all know the plan, do it often enough. Quarter the
fell, line search, meanwhile there's Ann and Rusty going
to where the lady was last seen, going up the lane from
her house towards the stone path, though the rain won't
help Rusty with the scent and Rob doubts anyone really
thinks the lady's just sitting on the track. Kate, she's
called. Not the same, Miro asks, because they were out for
a Kate two weeks ago, but it's not, there are just a lot of
women called Kate now of an age to go off alone and get
themselves into difficulties. He and Miro clip on their
radios, turn on the headtorches, heft the rucksacks and set
off up the track. Raindrops fall like sparks in the torchlight, and inside his hood there's the noise of rain on
waterproofs, the rasp of arms and legs in dense layers, the
splash of boots through puddles. Lisa's talking to him but
he can't hear, pushes his hood back, what? I said, she
says, isn't it your turn with Ellie? Aye, he says, yes, but
she's old enough now, she's only to eat her dinner and go
to bed, I told her we're down half the team but she doesn't
get it. Ah, she'll understand when she's older, Lisa says,
but he's not sure about that, it's not as if Liz ever under-
stood, always acted as if a call-out was a party invitation,
as if he was off down the pub rather than up the hills in

all weathers when she wanted him on the sofa with her in front of the TV all night or taking Ellie out at the weekend so she could have 'me time'. Time for what, he always wondered, because whatever it was left no discernible trace, nothing dirtier or cleaner than before, nothing new produced, no change in the appearance of Liz or the house where the me time had passed. Funny how it's only women get me time but even then he knew better than to say that out loud. Call-outs are mostly evenings and weekends, that's how it works, gets towards dusk and the families start wondering where people are, wait a bit, try phoning but everyone knows reception's dodgy on the hills, eat their dinner, try again and Dad's still not back, give it an hour, they still can't make contact and they make the emergency call right around the time you put kids to bed. Weekends are when folk who don't know what they're doing head up there and call 999 when they get cold and lost and scared, or folk who do know what they're doing run out of luck, fall or have a heart attack. Not that Rob reckons it's always bad luck, when it's his time that's how he wants to go, not the falling, horrible for everyone, but a proper conclusive MI on top of a mountain, preferably on his own so there isn't some poor sod attempting CPR on his cooling corpse. There's no point, in the mountains, you're always more than ten minutes from a defib which means that however good your technique a patient who's not breathing is dead and staying that way, but it doesn't stop people trying. Ben gets it now, Lisa says, he's even a bit proud of his old mum sometimes, it just takes time, teenagers aren't known for thinking of others. Yeah, he says, hope so.

He pulls the hood back up, but there's already rain running down his neck, trickling into the T-shirt under his fleece. Fair enough, November in the Peak District, what do you expect, but there's no denying it's a bad night, a bad night to get lost.

lonely road

HE PROMISED ALICE he'd keep the lights on, make himself some tea, stay busy. Watch a film, she said, something gentle you've seen before, and keep warm, won't you, I know your mum doesn't like to run the boiler but there's a time and a place, you know how to turn it on, don't you? And give me your number, I have your mum's but not yours, then I can at least check how you're doing. Wait, I've a great big batch of cookies here, let me give you some, you'll be doing me a favour, can you believe I had them instead of my dinner, at my age? I was going to send them to the grandchildren but you know how the post is these days, they'd be blue mouldy before they got there. Oh Matt, it feels so wrong to leave you standing there in the wet, you know I'd bring you inside in a heartbeat. You shouldn't be alone this evening, it's not right. Wait, I'll put some on a plate. Don't do that, he said, even if I wash it I'd have to touch it to give it back to you. Keep your cookies, Alice, you can freeze them or summat can't you?

I can, she said, but I'm going to give them to you, stay there. So now he has a foil parcel of cookies but he feels sick, he doesn't want anything to eat, wishes he hadn't had that omelette.

He takes off his mask, puts it in the washing machine, washes his hands, takes off his shoes and hangs up his coat. He checks his phone, there in the dark hall, but he doesn't want to tell anyone what's happening, that his mum has broken quarantine and Alice called the police and they're looking for her. Mountain rescue, whatever. Do they use mountain rescue for hunting criminals? There's no way Mum can afford the fine, isn't it like twenty grand or something, she doesn't earn that much in a year, what if she goes to prison, how will someone who can't even stay in her own house, who needs to be out the hills every day no matter the weather, survive prison? (How will he, for the matter of that, manage without her, would they make him go to his dad?) And what is she doing up there anyway, she doesn't stay out this long, not in the dark, what if she's hurt? Was she upset, that police-woman asked him, would you say your mum was distressed, Matt? I don't know, he said, thinking probably, maybe, but how's he supposed to know, they didn't talk about it and maybe he should have done, maybe he should have asked her. Isn't everyone distressed these days, isn't everyone supposed to be distressed? She's not been doing anything like the mental health girls at school, cutting themselves and crying and all that. Has she been behaving differently at all, the last few days, the woman kept on. Well yeah, he said, I mean, self-isolating, it's all been different, but normally she'd be up the moor or in the woods like every day. Walking, I mean, staying local, she follows the rules. Did, until now, I know she shouldn't— She's been tidying up, that was weird, not that we live in squalor or anything, I mean the house is clean, but she's not like one of those – yeah, that was different. She was getting rid of loads of stuff, clothes and that. The policewoman paused at that, as if decluttering is a symptom of summat. (It is, Mum would say, would normally have said, it's a symptom of buying too much crap, it's a symptom of late capitalism.) I'm sorry I have to ask you this, Matt, but because she hasn't seen anyone else for a while I do have to ask you, has your mum ever talked about feeling very low, about wanting to hurt herself? Have you checked if she left you a note?

That's what he needs to do. She does sometimes leave notes, if she's going out without her phone, which she does because she doesn't really like phones, says she doesn't need global tech corporations monitoring her from her pocket day and night, she knows how to read a real paper map with her own two eyes and we all get to be out of contact sometimes, even single parents. But she leaves the notes on Post-its on his computer screen, or sometimes on the back of an envelope against the kettle, and he'd have found it earlier, but he goes to check anyway, foot-steps loud on the stairs, and then he puts all the kitchen lights on and has a proper look, around the kettle and the countertops, goes through the pile of stuff by the fruit bowl, letters about the furlough payment thing while the café's closed and catalogues of clothes Mum can't afford, not that she'd have left a note there but it could have been moved somehow, and he does find one but it's from before, from last month, and it says 2pm Gone for walk Mam Tor − Rushup, back by dusk, pls bring in laundry if rain, lots of love Mum xxx. He remembers that day, Mum was back before him and the laundry got soaked because he went to the park with Jake and some of the others after school, outside, only five of them and OK probably not two metres apart but they're not two metres apart in the classroom either, and they still got yelled at by a woman who said they were sitting too close to each other and it was dis-gusting the way young people— Don't let it get to you, Jake said, they just hate us because we're not going to die and we're not scared of catching it, but in point of fact they are going to die, just probably later than old people, of whatever is around killing people in fifty years or whenever, and he is a bit scared and it does get to him, occasionally.

He checks his phone again. The policewoman said she'd call, as soon as there was news. Try not to worry, she said, they'll have a great team out there looking for her, she maybe just got lost, you said she's used to going up there so she knows how to keep safe, your neighbour saw her warmly dressed. We'll hope she's sheltering somewhere, won't we, keeping warm and waiting, but we'll have news soon. She wouldn't get lost, he said, she knows the fell, she's up there all the time, even sometimes at night and she carries a headtorch, a good one, I gave it to her one Christmas. It was one of his better presents, that torch, the first year he worked out that even though Mum's rude about Middle Aged Men In Lycra and all the high-tech stuff some people take to go for a walk, she likes kit, thermal gloves and socks and things for gardening, all biodegradable and organic and that. I know you like the dark in the woods, he said, but you can use it for walking on the road, or even if you wanted to do gardening at night. The torch has a solar charger as well as a USB, though admittedly the days on which you'd want a torch in these parts don't overlap much with the days when the sun would charge it.

He reads the old note again. Explaining where she was going, lots of love. She wouldn't leave him, not on purpose. What if there was some weirdo out there? There was a man living in an old caravan in the wood by Mortons' field last year, that was pretty creepy, he never opened the curtains and the van was all covered in moss and there were piles of rubbish. Mum felt sorry for him, which is exactly the problem, she never thinks anyone's bad. There but for the grace of God, she says, and if she did meet a weirdo on a lonely road at night she'd probably stop for a chat and invite him back for tea.

The phone rings and he nearly drops it, number withheld. Yes, he says, yes, hello. Is that Matthew, yes he says, what, tell me. It's the policewoman and the kitchen blurs and fades but she says there's no news, Matt, nothing yet, I just wanted you to know they've got four teams out there now and a search dog and they'll bring in the helicopter soon, the coastguard helicopter because of the weather, so we're doing everything, OK, and we'll find her for you, Matt, we'll find your mum, but you do know we can't say what state she'll be in, we'll hope for good news. Are you doing OK? We wouldn't leave you there on your own, normally, you'd have someone with you, is there at least someone you can talk to, a family member maybe on Face-Time or whatever? What about your dad? No, he says, I'm all right, thanks, and I'm sorry, I'm really sorry, about the people, I mean, and the helicopter, I know it's expensive, Mum would have never wanted to cause trouble, she's not like that, I know she shouldn't have gone out, she's just an outdoor person, she was in the garden but maybe it wasn't enough. Never mind that, says the policewoman, Joanne. Resource allocation isn't your job, all right? Let's find her before we worry about anything else. I'm going to update you every so often, all right, so don't think there's necessarily news when you see this number. You sure there's no one else we should call? No, he says, no, thank you, there's no one, I'm OK.

We'll hope for good news. He's being prepared, he realises, for bad news.

Holding the phone in his hand, he goes through to the front room. There's Mum's blanket on the sofa and he wraps it around his shoulders, sits down and waits.

not reading

ALICE GOES TO bed. She might as well. Electric blanket, book, but she keeps realising she's moving her eyes along the lines, turning the pages, not reading. It's nice enough, being warm and comfortable, but she can almost feel Matt through the wall, feel his fear. And Kate, out there on a night like this, you could almost feel her too, on the wind and the rain, in the dark. There's nothing she can do, she reminds herself, which could be the motto of the last six months, and the way things are looking also the next six months, and who knows about the six months after that. A person can doubtless live like this indefinitely, the background murmur of dread only a little louder week by week, month by month – well, that's obvious, isn't it, people don't die of dread, nor even imprisonment, or at least they do but not directly from being shut away, from lack of access to healthcare and poor diet and suicide and violence and many of the reasons that put them there in the first place, shame on her for comparing her comfy house, mortgage paid off, with her kind neighbours and her garden, to a prison. It's been years since she did the visiting scheme, Mark never really liked her driving off there, coming back, he said, with the smell of the place on her clothes, but she kept it up for years and you don't forget what a prison is like. No electric blankets, that's for sure. No trees through the windows, no home-made cookies. I'm just glad, one man said, that I can see the sky, because I can look up at the clouds and think that if my kids are looking up they might be seeing the same ones, I know the moon's shining on them the same as on me. It was always surprising, disturbing, that the people in there were so much like the people out here. You'd think, she'd thought, Mark probably went on thinking, that criminals are different from the rest of us, hardened or something – well, by the time they came out, maybe – but it wasn't so. There were plenty of people who'd got caught doing stuff only incrementally worse than what most of us chance, maybe not burglary or assault but speeding, a little shoplifting, cash-in-hand to a builder, she's done all of those herself though the last shoplifting was years ago, Susie in the pram and she never even knew why she did it, just the odd packet of expensive ham in the supermarket, a lipstick she had no reason to wear, little luxuries they couldn't afford and didn't need and she'd never done it before and never did it again once Susie was old enough that she might have noticed. It was the risk, maybe, spice in a life that had contracted to the baby and the house, the possibility of being seen when she was otherwise invisible. Anyway there but for the grace of God, she understands how you might steal even what you don't need. There was one man she thought about for years afterwards, a vicar who'd been on bad terms with his neighbour and was finally goaded into losing his temper while trimming the hedge with gardening shears. At least it wasn't a chainsaw, he'd said, but she'd thought that if it had been five minutes later when he'd have been sweeping up the clippings, or five minutes after that holding maybe a newspaper or a biscuit— And plenty of lads in for much less than that, lads who didn't have the vicar's manners or legal representation, in the wrong place at the wrong time doing something daft and possibly dangerous but rarely evil. And also, of course, some properly mad scary blokes you really wouldn't want to meet on the outside, though doubtless some properly mad scary things had happened to them somewhere along the way to make them like that. And so, Alice thinks, let us give thanks for our pure blind luck as well as our warm beds and safe houses, though the problem with giving thanks for your own luck is that you're also giving thanks that the misfortune landed on someone else. Keep a gratitude journal, says Kathleen, it's a big help, reminds you how lucky you are, and Alice thought grateful to whom, exactly, and for what, that my very ordinary virtues have been disproportionately rewarded in this world while worse things happen to better people? (Maybe this kind of thought, this kind of riposte, is one of the reasons she isn't a better person. Mark loved her though, didn't he, all those years?)

She opens out her legs and arms, starfish, for the warmth across the bed and for the space of it. She does miss Mark, still sometimes reaches for him in the night, always will, you don't just get over forty-five years of shared life, but you have to notice the small pleasures, otherwise what hope is there?

she'd have been

KATE, THEY'RE SHOUTING, Kate! His torch sweeps the wet heather, shows it lacy and black in silver rain, meets the beam of Miro's torch, sweeps back. Rob thinks of all the names he's called across the moor these last ten years, all the names drifting in the troubled air. They find people, that's not really the problem, the fell's not so big and between the four teams you can walk pretty much all of it, at least come daylight, it's not like the Alps or even Scotland where sometimes they just have to trust to the mountain and time to take care of the ones who won't be coming home. It's only that naturally you don't always find people in time. Sometimes it was too late before you were called, sometimes it was probably too late by the time they set foot on the path, the day's end determined by decisions taken last night or last week or by a parent's abuse or the failure of a marriage years in the past. Swiss cheese, they call it: every slice has a couple of holes but it's only when you line them up and the holes overlap that there's a problem. On most walks probably someone forgot their waterproof or the weather turns unexpectedly or their friend cancelled at the last minute so they went out alone or the route they planned is impossibly muddy so they take the long way or they were delayed leaving and have less daylight in hand than you'd want but as long as those things are *or* and not *and* you're OK. God knows they've all done it, one thing forgotten leading to one small but in retrospect unwise decision and then some unexpected change of circumstances, usually weather, magnifying the poor decision or the forgetting and suddenly you can see how this could all go really badly wrong but mostly you're lucky, mostly it doesn't. You get away with it. That time in Glencoe: late start for no particular reason, maybe an extra pint the night before, maybe just folk being scatty in the morning; Stu's knee playing up, he could keep going but they were slower than usual; his own waterproof forgotten at a rest stop and remembered after they'd gone up something they couldn't go down, all manageable and then the weather closes in a few hours earlier than forecast and they're colder, slower, higher up and later than they ought to be and it all starts to look a bit serious. You do some silent bargaining with a God you don't believe in before you make it back to the pub but you're not scared enough to keep your end of the deal once you're warm and dry. Ice-climbing in Llanberis, two years ago, dropped an ice axe that should have been tied on, they were fucking lucky to get away with that one. This lady, though, Kate, he doesn't like the story: she's setting off far too late for someone who knows what she's doing, she's alone, she doesn't take her phone and she's been having a bad time lately. You'd like to think that having kids would stop people killing themselves but it doesn't, probably by the time someone's in that state they can no more think of others and keep going than a person with cancer or heart disease can think of others and recover by force of will. Kate, he shouts, Kate!

The path gets steeper here, up Blackshaw Clough, and they're coming to the rocks where people sometimes fall, though in Rob's opinion, from what the lad apparently said, he reckons Kate would have gone straight on, Crowden way, not along the main trail but out over the tops on the path that's not signed, and then if she's fallen it's likely not off the edge – she knows the place too well for that – but somewhere towards the Woolpacks, where you have to keep jumping the streams and picking your way over bogs and in falling light not to mention rain it's easy enough to sprain your ankle however well you know the land. That's where he'd have gone, Rob, if he'd been stuck in a house for ten days and couldn't take another minute of it, if he'd seen the dusk and known it was past time to turn back but couldn't, not quite yet, couldn't go back to airless little rooms and other people, even one other person, always in hearing, always about to want something. Unless, that's to say, things had got so bad he felt the pull of Cluther Rocks, Kinder Downfall, about the only place hereabouts where one decisive step could be relied on to be final, it's not that he's never thought about it, what he would do if it came to that, hasn't everyone thought about it sometime or other, but not round here, you don't want it to be your mates picking up the pieces. Into the sea, he'd always thought, would be better, tidy yourself up as you go, but this is about as far from the sea as you can get and he doubts offing yourself neatly counts as an 'essential purpose' for travel when you could perfectly well do it in the confines, in the confinement, of your own house. It's like trying to keep a wolf in the house, living with you, Liz used to say, you're not housetrained, you're barely even tame, and she wasn't right or kind – he's always kept stuff clean and tidy, she was the messy one – but she wasn't exactly wrong either. He gets it, why you'd run away. You shouldn't – it's costing a fortune, all this PPE, having to disinfect everything every time anyone touches it, not to mention it's against the law and she's risking a huge fine, not to mention she's supposed to be isolated for a reason and if any of the team gets sick they'll all be close contacts and then there isn't much of a mountain rescue service at all for two weeks given how many are already off – but he gets why you would. As long as that's all it is, running away. Kate, he shouts, Kate!

Rain batters his shoulders and hood, and the grass underfoot is slippery with water. On hands and feet up here, better safe than sorry. Sweat trickles on Rob's back, but he knows the temperature's dropping. If Kate's not moving she could be getting pretty cold by now. Wait, says Miro, there's something — nah, sorry, sheep. The sheep stares over its shoulder at their lights, bleats, can't quite be bothered to get up and run away. They're coming up to the top now, the point where Kate probably meant to turn back, because if she had, and if nothing happened to her on the way down, she'd have been back to the lane not much after dusk, well able to find her way home, and she'd have worked her legs and lungs a bit, seen out over the tops where she used to walk all day, got back to her quarantine with no one the wiser. The cloud seems to be closing in up here, lying over the tops. It's not ideal, fog. It won't make anything easier.

you would end up

COLD WINTER WAS howling o'er moor and o'er mountain – breathe – and wild was the surge of the dark rolling sea. Kate's voice wavers. She can't breathe properly, not well enough to sing. I met about daybreak – breathe – a bonnie young lassie, who asked me the road – she has to breathe again – and the miles to Dundee. One more verse, and then she's going to move again, open the rucksack, because there's nothing in the first-aid kit that will mend a broken leg and whatever is wrong with the bad arm, but there are some painkillers that might take the edge off, maybe enough that she can start making her way down, back to Matt, because it's going to take a long time to get back to Matt, even to Breck End, crawling. The important thing is not to stop, not to go to sleep. Says I, my young lassie I cannae well tell ye, the road and the distance I cannae well give. But if ye'll permit me to gang a wee bittie, I'll show ye the miles and the road to Dundee. She used to sing this one in pubs, with Tom and his fiddle, the sort of pubs where you finish with The Manchester Rambler and it turns into a singsong, feet stamping under the tables. I'm a rambler, I'm a rambler, from Manchester way, I get all me pleasure the hard moorland way. I may be a wage slave on Monday, but I am a free man on Sunday.

And she's here again, the second voice. Hello Raven, she says, you came back! Sing with me, Raven. What do ravens sing? Remember o thou man, o thou man. You're lucky, no one's tried to stop the birds singing, people keep talking about the war the way they always talk about the war but music was allowed, wasn't it, encouraged, even, Vera Lynn and singalongs in bomb shelters though I dare say all that's exaggerated, probably plenty of whimpering and swearing going on as well. Bless 'em all, bless 'em all, the long and short and the tall. We'll get no promotion this side of the ocean, so cheer up my lads bless 'em all. Her grandfather used to sing that one, his bass voice always surprising from a small man, shorter than her by the time she was twelve but he was also a bit bow-legged, rickets, not enough to eat in the back streets of Sheffield in the 1920s, bread and a scraping of marge, he used to say, jam on Sundays, no wonder he grew his own veg as soon as he had a garden. Wouldn't talk about the war, not even in the last year before he died when he didn't know which month it was but came out with all sorts she'd never heard before about his childhood, haunting, some of it, can't say there hasn't been progress even if it's all going backwards now, but he taught them the songs, her and the cousins, bowdlerised of course she realised later, driving over the Dark Peak, no seatbelts in those days, her and Gary and Danielle, belting it out from the black plastic back seat, could get wicked hot in summer, shorts and bare thighs. They say there's a troop-ship just leaving Bombay. Ravens, battlefields. You're not waiting for me to die, are you? To peck my eyes? I've seen you at dying lambs, Raven, your kind. Your unkind.

But the raven, she thinks, probably could peck her eyes, ravens are big and even the good arm doesn't lift far. If that's what the raven's here for. You can't blame birds. Painkillers, that's what she was after. In the green first-aid kit, in the rucksack, not many because she taped up the fatal dose and locked it in the car. Kate tries to push herself up. No, try rolling. Well, it will hurt, won't it? That's why you need the tablets. Remember o thou man. This must be it. There's rain in her eyes. Good clean rain. Little Kate was out on the fells in the Chernobyl rain, thirty years ago. They killed all the sheep, afterwards, radioactive sheep, inedible, untouchable, and the poison seeping into the ground and also into her and her brother's skin and hair, into muscle and blood and bone. Well but we didn't know, her mum said, I was never all that interested in the news, you know that. Doesn't mean the news isn't interested in you, the point of being interested in the news is that sometimes you can see it coming before it's at your door. The point of the news is that you know how to vote and when to take to the streets, not that her mother did either. The sheep, the mink, foot and mouth, animals burnt and ploughed into the ground, contaminated, poisoned blood and poisoned soil. Open the first-aid kit. She holds it in the good hand, feels with her lips for the zip, takes it in her teeth, cold, pulls, feels the ripple of metal through her skull. Don't let things fall out, don't leave the plasters and the antiseptic for the sheep and birds to eat, and here they are, she cut up the blister pack, only four and the rest in the car. Two for now, then, two more for later. She sucks her damp hair for moisture to help her swallow them. Give it twenty minutes, then she's going to find the torch and set off.

She lets the first-aid kit fall and lies back under the foil blanket. She wants her duvet. She wants her bed. She wants the pain to stop.

Rain drums on the blanket and there's a rush of wings, a rude raven remark. Not my eyes, she says. *King Lear*, she thinks, the old man on the cliff. She took Matt to see it in Sheffield a few years ago, somehow forgot that it's not only computer games and films that need age ratings. You think Shakespeare's going to be suitable, don't you, improving, and it probably was but Matt had nightmares for weeks. Vile jelly. It was very realistic, not that she's seen anyone have their eyes pulled out, of course. Leave me be, Raven. Matt, says the raven, you left him. You didn't tell him you were going out.

No, she thinks, if you're going to be my conscience or my guardian angel or something, if I'm stuck on a mountainside for the night with the voice of judgement, I'd rather you just pecked out my eyes. Probably. If you'd brought your phone you could have called him, says the raven. How do you think he's feeling now, alone, can't even leave the house, doesn't know where you are? Not to mention you could have called for help.

I don't want help, she says, I'm helping myself. I couldn't call anyone, I'm not supposed to be here.

Helping yourself? Off the mountain? What, with headache tablets and folk songs? Sorry but how far exactly do you think you've gone, and in how long?

This isn't how she thinks of ravens. She should never have sung with it, given it delusions of grandeur.

And you realise, don't you, you're going to need medical attention for that leg, it's not something you can sort out yourself with a day in bed and some aromatherapy?

She's never said aromatherapy works for broken bones, or cancer. None of that. It just makes you feel better sometimes, that's all, if you've a cold or a stomach upset, a headache, sadness or sorrow. Anyway maybe the leg isn't broken.

Oh, there's going to be sadness and sorrow all right. Because you'll need treatment and you'll have to tell the doctor you're supposed to be in quarantine, won't you, supposing they don't already know which they probably do, you'll have a number and it'll come up on the screen and then what? Trouble, that's what. If you'd just stayed at home the way you were told none of this would have happened. And of course it's broken, why else do you think it's not working?

Go away, Kate thinks, bugger off. Are you a spirit guide or my mother? Oh God what if it's both. Remember o thou man, she sings, o thou man, o thou man. Remember o thou man, thy time is near. There's another wave of pain, but maybe slightly dulled by the pills. Or not.

She's had her rest. Time to set off, down the hill, which would be easier if she knew exactly where she was, exactly what she'd fallen off, if she could remember what had happened. Down, anyway, is the answer to which way, and wherever she comes to the valley she'll recognise it, and know how to go home. The raven caws and she hears wings over her head. What, you're planning to crawl along the road? In the dark? And what about the rucksack, hm, are you leaving it on the hillside or were you planning to get it onto your damaged back using your arms that don't work so you can add to the weight on your broken leg as you drag yourself along? Since I could get to the rucksack, she thinks, I can go a few metres and if I go a few metres enough times it will be a lot of metres and maybe I'll be able to get home before someone catches me out here, breaking quarantine, going out on the hills alone and late in the day and without a phone at the arse end of the year, doing a remarkably good impression of someone rather stupid. Hush now, no point in that, there'll be time enough for recrimination. Get down the mountain and then worry about the other problems.

She feels for the rucksack. The raven's not wrong. She can't put it on, let alone carry it. So she should drink the water and eat the Fig Rolls and probably try to use the bandages in the first-aid kit because that's what they're for, isn't it, that's why she's been carrying bandages up and down mountains for the last twenty years and there's a sling in there as well, a crisp square of unbleached linen but how could a person put a sling on herself, not to mention it wouldn't help with the crawling. Leg, she thinks, bandage the leg, remembering that proper rock-climbing man who crawled down the Andes with bones sticking out of his trousers, at least she's not at the bottom of a crevasse, at least she doesn't have to cross a glacier, at least she won't have to travel slung across a donkey for several days before she can see a doctor, assuming that seeing a doctor is worth being found out, assuming that doctors are even still seeing people who break quarantine. How much is the fine, anyway, though however much it is she can't afford it and she'd rather have an untreated fracture than risk prison, even more stupid to end up in prison because you couldn't bear being locked up at home than to go get yourself into trouble on the fells when you should know better, when you're leaving your son – this isn't going to help. And she's getting cold, and maybe this isn't going to work, this whole ridiculous idea, because the pain is really – the pain recalibrates the idea of pain. Shingles, sinusitis, kidney infection, childbirth, she's always thought, in that order, and most of childbirth was perfectly manageable, it was just some of the last bit. She tries to move the leg again, to see what it's like, which is a mistake.

Another mistake, says the raven, shall we make a list? We could go all the way back, couldn't we, tell me, Kate, what was the first mistake you ever made, would you say? What poor choice set you on the path to where we find ourselves this evening? School, she thinks, school was all mistakes, though whether this night was determined by the time I left school – Raven, you're not my mother, you're Miss Boucher, aren't you, Miss Boucher who told me off in front of the whole canteen on my first day because my shoes were the wrong colour and she wasn't interested in my weird duck-feet and my mother's admittedly hereditary last-minute approach to matters such as shopping for school uniform, it's as if both of us and probably now poor Matt as well think that if we ignore for example Christmas or summer or the beginning of the school year it might go away and we won't after all need presents or sunscreen or the right shoes, which isn't entirely mad because the end is nigh, we do know that, and if we're all about to die in a nuclear war or that one

where the magnetic poles swivel which she always imagines as the planet flipping, Australia at the top and
Greenland at the bottom and all the fuses in the world
blowing like fireworks as the planet spins through the
darkness, or a more conclusive plague than the current
slow-burning one or any of the many other reasons for the
streets to run with blood, who wants to have spent their
last days of ignorant normality looking for navy lace-up
shoes in a size 2H? Though one of the things we're learning, we of the end times, is that humanity's ending
appears to be slow, lacking in cliffhangers or indeed any
satisfactory narrative shape; characterised, for the lucky,
by the gradual vindication of accumulating dread, which
is entirely compatible with and sometimes a motive for
buying stuff, as though the obvious response to global
overheating is to have more kinds of sunscreen and
UV-protective T-shirts rather than for example not using
fossil fuels. She's thought before, never mind A-levels,
Matt ought to be learning organic farming and metal-
smithing and spinning and weaving, the next generation
needs pre-industrial skills. Not that she was interested in
gardening at his age, so maybe there's time, except that
time is what there isn't, time's what's running short,
except that people have thought that before and they were
wrong, which doesn't mean that everyone who thinks it's
the end times will always be wrong.

So these survival skills, the raven asks, would they

include saving yourself when you've fallen on the hill, or were you just planning to lie here and succumb to hypothermia, shock and accumulating dread?

That's not fair, she says, weren't you just mocking my plan to go home? I'm not succumbing, that's the whole point, if I was going to succumb I'd be asleep by now. I'm resisting. I'm fighting. I'm just taking a short rest. I'm pacing myself.

Quite a long rest, the raven says, compared to how long you actually spent moving. Kate lacks motivation, isn't that what they used to say? Disorganised and no respect for authority?

Respect for authority is dangerous, she says, how do you think totalitarian governments work? How much does authority respect you, Raven, or me or any of us? And I have motivation, enough motivation to get out of bed every morning and get Matt off to school and go to work and come home and do the shopping and the cooking and pay the bills, that's not nothing, that's actually a whole lot, day after day, year after year. I sing. I do gardening. I'm even on the Parish Council. Not at the moment, the raven says, none of that. No, she says not at the moment, no.

So, shall we try again? What brings us here this evening? What poor decisions, Kate, what ill-advised acts, set you on this path? At what point in your life, Kate, would you say it became inevitable that you would end up criminal, alone and injured on a mountain in the dark?

Stop saying my name like that, she says. It's not relevant, inevitability, it won't help. I need to keep moving. And I haven't ended up and it's not, by the way, technically a mountain.

The raven makes a raven sound. It is perfectly obvious what she means.

Kate uses the good arm to move the bad one and rolls back towards the rucksack, trying to stay under the blanket. She makes a noise again. She gets the good hand into the bag. Not water, she doesn't need to be working out how to pee. A Fig Roll is probably a good idea if she can get it down. Work the painkillers into her coat pocket, never mind the other things, we're beyond elastic bandages, and the plasters and antiseptic cream speak rather sweetly of moments at which a cut finger is a problem of significance. Rain's running off the foil blanket into her jeans. The shaking is starting again, but here's the headtorch, and if she can fasten the strap one-handed, holding it against the ground with her skull, she's ready to go.

he hears the helicopter

MATT'S LOOKED AT everything on the internet and everyone's asleep and nothing's changing. He didn't think you could do that, reach the point where nothing's updated since you last looked, he thought the whole point of the internet was that it could eat your entire life, that you could just go round and round perpetually scrolling because there is no rest, and he could of course start reading stuff he's not interested in but he's not going to. He lies back against the sofa cushions, rolls his shoulders. Something crunches. You need yoga, Mum would say, but she thinks everyone needs yoga. It's so cold. He pulls the blanket up over his head, sits hooded. Cup of tea, he supposes. They will find her, won't they? They promised to find her. He can't remember ever hearing that they gave up without finding the person, but he knows, because you can't live round here, you can't go to his school or be in the football team where he used to play or drink where he was starting to drink and not know, that not everyone they bring down is alive. And if Mum's not — he didn't think this would ever happen, it's all wrong, for it to be the kid sitting at home worrying about the mum, he doesn't know how to do this. It was stupid of her not to take her phone, what's the point in having a phone if you're always leaving it when you go out. It was stupid of her to go out, she could have waited, couldn't she, another week, kept skipping and digging the garden and leaving her yoga mat all over the sitting room, plenty of people don't go for walks from one month to the next, and if she was going to go for a walk the least she could have done was to tell him. What if that policewoman's right, asking all the questions about Mum's mood, feeling low and all that? Of course she's been low, who wouldn't be, who isn't? Doesn't mean everyone's offing themselves and anyway going for a walk, with a rucksack, with warm clothes and a torch and a first-aid kit, isn't an obvious way to go about it, not that there aren't places you could jump, if that's what you wanted, not that people don't jump, sometimes, but you wouldn't dress for the weather and carry a compass and a survival blanket, would you? And Mum wouldn't, anyway, she just wouldn't. She likes what she does too much, singing and walking and her friends and even working in the café. None of which she's been able to do since— He's always thought he'd stand in front of a train, if it came to it, they pass just above the village and there are a couple of paths that cross the line, easy enough. Something fast and violent, anyway, something where you can't change your mind.

He's still cold. He stands up, stiff, wraps the blanket around his shoulders. He wants to be in his bed knowing Mum's in hers where she ought to be. He wants to wake up and find that none of this is real. Carrying his phone, he goes down the hall to the kitchen, where nothing has changed, where the bare trees still peer in from the dark. He could clean, he supposes, Mum'd like to come back and find the place clean, not that it's dirty, got cleaned on Saturday in the usual way but it was his turn to do the kitchen and he knows fine well he doesn't do it the way Mum does. It's so pointless, cleaning the kitchen, lasts about two hours before the next meal. He turns the lights on, hears the thud from upstairs as the cat jumps off his bed to come and see what's happening. Start by putting away the stuff on the draining board so he can wash the omelette pan so he can dry that and put it away as well. It's not the cleaning he really hates, it's the way you have to move all this random stuff around loads of times before you can even start.

He's trying to fit the colander into the pans in the cupboard, because there's only one way of doing it that means you can close the cupboard door and Mum thinks it's obvious but it's bloody not, every single time he has to take everything out, when he hears the helicopter. It's low and although he's not sure he wants to see any of this, might rather not have heard, he runs upstairs to watch its light paint the fell. You can feel the noise in the joists of the house, in your bones.

come the hour

THE HOUSE SHAKES. Gales, Alice thinks, thunder. She must have slept, because the book is flat on her chest and whatever she read last, it's not in her mind now. Oh, it's the helicopter out there, and if the helicopter's out it means they still haven't found Kate. What time is it? That's not good. That means it's – nine, ten, eleven – over five hours since she saw Kate going up the lane. If only she'd called out, opened a window and shouted, persuaded her not to go, to remember Matt and the wretched rules and stay home just a few more days, to spend the time maybe planning the walks she'll do later, when all this is over, not even necessarily round here, a proper holiday, the Highlands, Snowdonia or the Lakes. Not that it always helps to plan, sometimes just makes you feel worse because you know you're lying to yourself imagining future fun, except that the bad feeling is also a lie because if you really knew for sure that nothing's going to change you wouldn't plan. It's not-knowing we hate, even though we never know, even though a man can be, so to speak, full of vigour and the joys of spring when he wakes beside his wife of forty-five years one fine April morning and dead by lunchtime, even though that wife can feel entirely well while the cells in her left breast go forth and multiply in ways they should not. It was never safe to plan, we just used to be able to pretend otherwise. But that, of course, is the one thing we do know: death. Oh, not this one again, it's not interesting or clever. Think about something else. Baking, the recipe in the weekend paper, hazelnuts. Where to go on holiday, who to invite to a party, when all this is over. If all this is ever— oh, shut up. One day the mind thinking this thought will end. One day there will be no Alice. These hands here under the duvet will fall still and cold and begin to rot, these eyes— stop it, this was tedious enough when you were fourteen. What if she's frightened, come the hour, the hour which is nearer now than it was when she started this thought, the hour that's been coming since her first breath, inevitable, waiting, what if it's actually terrifying, what if she goes out in undignified horror? Well, she thinks, what then, if you can't make a fool of yourself when you're dead then really what hope is there? It's not as if she'll have to cope with the consequences.

The helicopter's coming back, and she gets out of bed to stand in front of the curtain and watch, as if she might be able to see if they've found Kate. Maybe it's going away, the job done, though it could be another call-out, but no, it's following the line of the lane up to Breck End. They surely don't think Kate's there, on the road? And now the people at Breck End will know that Kate went out, across their land, and soon it'll be all over the village. Poor Matt. She watches the lights crossing the sky, thinks she can maybe see torches on the hillside. Hunting, she thinks, and calls it back. Rescuing, not hunting. Poor Kate.

She opens the curtain so she can see out, goes back to bed and turns on the bedside light, piles up the pillows so she can sit comfortably. Glasses, phone. She finds Matt's number and writes to him: Hope you're holding up, just wanted to let you know that I'm awake and thinking of you and your mum. Knock on the door if you need anything! You're not alone, she adds, but then deletes it, creepy, maybe, not to mention untrue. Send. It's not decent, that the lad has to be on his own tonight. She's never asked much about the father, what's-his-name, seemed perfectly all right at the time but as Mark used to say at the end of a good gossip you never can tell about other people's marriages, Alice is pretty sure it was an affair rather than anything really nasty that ended things, even so you'd think if there was ever a time for a man to turn up and be a dad this would be it, quarantine or no. She gets up again, cranes in the window to see if there are any lights on next door. That poor lad. If he were any younger, she thinks, she'd put on a mask and gloves and go round there, at least sit with him, play cards or watch TV or whatever. Maybe if she were any younger, even if the cancer and its treatment were less recent. But it would be more stupid than brave, wouldn't it, to go now, after all these months of isolation? Shielding, they call it, silly military metaphors, first you have to battle cancer and then you have to shield from a virus, as if life was one of those wargames where there's nothing to do but kill or be killed. Seb showed her once, most of them don't even include food or sleep or going to the loo, let alone anything a person might do for fun. Yeah, Seb said, but have you thought that given how things are looking, the dystopia games might be more useful to me and my friends than going to the opera or whatever? Better preparation? Nonsense, the world's always been at war and the strange thing about the current pandemic isn't that it's happening now but that it didn't happen for so long. Humans could always hear the four horsemen if we listened for them, even in the Sixties which Seb imagines as one long party. Give or take the Cold War. Ignoring kids with polio, the Cuban Missile Crisis, not to mention the sheer bloody awfulness of being a woman, not being allowed contraception unless you were married, not being able to open a bank account without your husband's permission — immediately given, in her case, but that's not the point.

Here's the helicopter again. What is Kate playing at, going off on her own in the dark like that? It'll be costing a fortune, this search, the helicopter and the dogs and the rescue teams dragged out of their warm beds, and let's hope she's not contagious when they find her because they won't get her off the hill without touching her, breathing her breath. The village isn't going to like this, or at least the village will be enjoying the story and disapproving of Kate for weeks, months, there's been enough trouble about people cycling and going for walks perfectly within the rules, back in the spring there was someone stringing wire across the lanes at a height intended to match cyclists' necks, apparently intent on decapitation, wanting to see village lanes run with city-dwellers' blood, a self-defeating as well as medieval response to the fear of contagion since that blood's going to spread a lot more disease running in the streets than minding its own business inside someone's skin. We don't own the village, she wanted to say, half of you moved here to live in a National Park, did you never think about why it's called National, did you never hear of the Kinder Trespass, the whole point is supposed to be that these hills are for everyone. Not that there was a plague on during the Kinder Trespass, but plenty else to worry about then, between the wars, whenever. Oh and now she's sounding like Susie, judgemental old trout, if you're not going to sleep you should get up and do something, no point sitting here in your pillows condemning people. Usually she'd think she should stay where she is, the only way of weathering

these months is to make a routine and stick to it, otherwise she could easily be up all night and asleep all day,
having breakfast at midnight or more likely cake for
dinner and it won't do, that kind of thing, no need to
drive yourself crazy, you have to resist. If resisting isn't
another military metaphor, fighting the maddening times,
but if there's a war on hand probably better to be a
member of the resistance than the one with the big guns,
you'll probably like yourself better at the end, if you see
the end. What nonsense. Do something.

She should read her book, that's what it's there for, but
somehow she doesn't feel like it, not that you should be
governed by what you feel like, not at this hour of the
night at least. She stopped keeping the computer by her
bed, led to bad habits, but maybe just this once, this hard
night. Alice gets up again, puts on her slippers, turns on
the hall light to fetch her laptop from the desk in the sitting room. Back in bed, electric blanket pulled up under
her arms, she opens Private Browsing – no point having
people laugh at you when you die and they look at your
internet history – then the video site. The music starts and
the smiley Californian girl starts teaching you how to roller-
skate. You start in a park on a headland looking over the
Pacific, where the sun sets as you learn how to rise from
sitting on the ground wearing pink suede rollerboots.
Why should it occur to Roxi that there are parts of the
world where you'd catch your death of cold sitting on the

concrete, or get a wet backside or more than likely dog mess on your coat? Imagine living in a place where you can just sit on the ground like that! Feet in a V-shape, start by gently shifting your weight from one foot to the other, but after five minutes you can weave in circles, crossing your feet as you glide, and a couple of episodes later you're learning to go backwards down a steep hill in San Francisco, with pastel houses glowing in the sun and exotic American cars nosing the sidewalks, and you're wearing teeny little shorts and a T-shirt with the sleeves cut off and a sparkly helmet the colour of a tropical sea. Alice is saving the ones where you learn to jump and spin and dance, because winter is coming, winter on these clouded hills in these plague-riddled little islands.

Not that there isn't plague in California too, by now, maybe even more of it than here. But not in the rollerskating tutorials.

rock-climbing

ROB DOESN'T LIKE the way this is going. It shouldn't be taking so long, there wasn't long enough between Kate being seen going up the lane and sunset for her to have walked all the way out here, which means that either she kept going, kept walking away from her house and her son, for hours after nightfall with the weather closing in or they've missed her or she isn't on the fell at all, at which point you'd be wanting the police not mountain rescue. They're right up on the tops now, working along Sandy Heys, and the other team coming over Black Ashop Moor hasn't found a sign of her either. Kate, Miro's shouting, Kate! You just have to keep looking, follow the plan, doesn't matter what your ideas are, but you have ideas and his idea is that this woman is not where her story places her. Kate! Between the rain on his hood, the constant rhythm of waterproofs brushing heather, the wind, they could easily miss an answering shout.

He walks on. Of course he'd rather be with Ellie, that

part was true, but he likes it up here, sky and weather, the sense of the moor settled into the dark around him. Even at night, even in this weather, you can see the skyline, the curve of the moor darker than cloud. Folk do come up by night, the easy routes with headtorches, for the quiet and on a clearer night for the stars, always surprises him how many turn out to be roaming on a winter's night and sometimes the rock-climbers too and he gets that, he really does, because the point of rock-climbing is the concentration, the way your whole world contracts to the next move, the next reach, and so doing it in the dark is kind of obvious. Your headtorch shows you everything that matters, which is your hands and feet, but anyway it's not really about what you can see, more what you can feel, how your fingers and toes know the rock, a kind of relationship between your body and the stone that honestly he can only really compare to having sex, good sex, the kind where you're acting on instinct and instinct is right, one move to the next, except with the high that comes with danger, with the constant and immediate risk of death. It's like fucking the rock, or fucking yourself on the rock, or something, rock-climbing in the dark. On a good night.

He hasn't done any – rock-climbing, he means, there was a bit of sex despite the lockdown, humans have needs pandemic or not – since last year. Since – since Stu, because it's one thing knowing people fall and die and he did know that, he's not stupid, you don't spend thirty years crawling up cliffs to be surprised by falling and dying, God knows he's been to more funerals than some people twice his age, and it's one thing picking up the pieces of people you don't know, which he does, a lot, because Stanage Edge is in this patch, but it's another thing to watch your mate slip, to hear the noise he makes on the way down and see the explosion of blood on the rock below, to be first on scene and to see immediately that the injury is incompatible with life, though you had breakfast together and he was planning to go home and finish off the bathroom job because the tiler walked out and the missus wanted it done. Turns out that's another thing entirely, which makes no sense, because the danger is what makes climbing fun, addictive even, and he's always thought that people including himself, including Stu, have the right to take risks when they know what they're doing, and at all those other funerals it was sad but it wasn't wrong, to be standing at the graves of climbers in their twenties and thirties and forties because they did know what they were doing, they looked the risks in the eye and took them because that's what you do, that's how you know you're alive. You take the risk and you take the consequences. Only it didn't feel like that, watching Stu die, and it didn't feel like that seeing Ciara and the kids at his funeral.

Kate, he calls, Kate!

Sometimes you get home and go to bed and wake yourself up shouting the person's name.

Miro's torch picks up movement but it's another sheep, affronted, hurrying away. He hears the helicopter coming back for another pass.

They should have found her by now.

this my comeuppance

FAREWELL, YE DUNGEONS dark and strong, the wretch's destiny. MacPherson's time will not be long, on yonder gallows tree. Kate's beginning to notice, behind the great pain of the leg and the lesser but not inconsiderable pains of the bad arm and the back, the feeling that her hair is being pulled, all the hair from ear to ear over the top, tightening. Oh what is death, but parting breath, on many a bloody plain. I've dared his face, and in this place, I'll dare him once again. A silly song to sing, no one's putting her in a dungeon. It should be easy, going downhill, but the problem – one of the problems – is that if she pushes herself along on her bottom the leg goes first and she can more or less drag it but she can't push it so she's crawling, head first, which means face in the heather, the torch showing her a hare's eye view though hares stand up to see over the heather. You see them up here, even in winter, lovely hares. Ach little did my mother think, when first she cradled me, that I would turn a roving boy, and die on the gallows tree. Kate's mother probably wouldn't be much surprised. You just don't learn to think ahead, do you Kate, consequences surprise you every time, we used to think you'd grow out of it, that if we let you make your own mistakes you'd learn from them.

She pushes up on the good arm, to see over the heather, and in the torchlight the raven's back, waiting for her on a rock. She's summoned it, she thinks, it was the mention of mistakes. That or the raven's circling her, the way they circle dying sheep, but not so far as Kate knows at night. Owls, there are some in the woods, often on night walks she hears their conversations and sometimes, if she's quiet and lucky, sees one, always in flight, a soft fleet shape on the dark sky. You'd never know what had happened, if an owl took you, wouldn't hear it coming. Maybe the raven's just guiding her down, showing the way. Sae rantonly, sae wantonly, sae dauntingly gaed he, he played a tune and danced it roon, by yonder gallows tree. The raven caws. Come on then, this way. Why are you with me, Raven, she asks, what are you doing here? Maybe ravens like night-flying, maybe she's out for fun, to see what's happening. Not in this weather. Kate's headache's getting worse. More pills, she thinks, but the idea of trying to get them out of her pocket is exhausting. Just make it to the raven, then she can pause. She pulls herself another step, and another. It hurts.

So, your first mistake, the raven says, have you thought

of it yet? Marrying Paul, she thinks, all the signs were there, no one really gets less annoying with time. If she hadn't married him she might have had a different kind of life, not been a single mum waitressing in her forties, not that there's anything wrong with waitressing but maybe if she'd waited she could have married someone with wider horizons or at least better clothes, a singer, Tom, she's sometimes thought, if Tom were single which he's not, so they just flirt a bit sometimes, chastely, nothing that should upset Mel, barely enough to give the music a little extra charge, but if she'd met Tom first, if she'd taken the singing more seriously before Matt was born, not that she could ever have made a living from it, folk music, hardly anyone – but still, yes, we can probably say, she tells the raven, that if I hadn't married Paul I wouldn't be here just now. She'd thought, she realises, that a man who didn't hit you, didn't lose his temper and use you as a punchbag, was a lovely person, and it's not that Paul wasn't a lovely person, probably, for someone else, only that it turns out you can't found a marriage on being grateful not to be beaten up, not when the person not beating you up is irritating and once you get used to not being beaten up you can't hide the irritation and eventually he gets sick of you being irritated and goes off and shags someone less irritable and by that stage it's kind of a relief all round, much easier to break up with someone because they're shagging someone else than because you can't stand their table manners and the way they dig at their scalp with their fingernails and actually you never liked the way they smell, not that Paul didn't wash but there was just something kind of sweet and ever so slightly rotten on his skin that had always been a turnoff. Don't marry someone whose smell doesn't turn you on, that's what she'd say now, if anyone asked which they won't. Don't marry someone who picks his ears in public, however nice he is. It won't get easier.

Right, says the raven, you didn't make a mistake until you were twenty-five?

Another pull.

Obviously, there was Billy, what Billy did, what she didn't stop him doing, not until it had gone on for months and she'd lied to everyone from the nurses in A and E to the man in the corner shop so often she'd forgotten how to tell the truth, and she knows it wasn't her fault, she's heard it, over and again, but that doesn't mean there weren't mistakes, ones she'll never make again. Also, maybe related because maybe if she'd had certificates, if she'd had a plan, maybe she'd have been less convinced by Billy at the beginning, maybe he wouldn't ever have seemed like the answer to the problem of her life, there was not working harder at school. Not seeing until it was too late that there were opportunities as well as adults on power trips at school, that it might have been worth going along with the power trips for the opportunities. Maybe never going back and doing an Access course or whatever for university, which she could have done, after Billy, probably even any time up until Matt was born, though Paul wouldn't have liked it. Not that having a degree seems to have made much difference to the lives of most of the graduates she knows, or at least only the younger ones and the difference there is the lifetime of debt, but she missed some stuff, and she could have maybe gone, at least tried to go, while there were still grants, Sheffield or Manchester, studied Ecology maybe or Forestry, that could have been a different life. So yes, mistakes: the two big relationships of her life, her education, the lack of a career, not to mention not being a great mum, not really understanding how to be a mum until it was probably too late because don't they say it's the first thousand days that determine the course of the child's life, Matt's future already damaged by her drinking coffee in pregnancy and crying when he had colic, not to mention not being a great daughter either, not to mention failing to cope with lockdown even though she hasn't been sick, hasn't lost anyone, and not only failing to cope but actually failing to isolate herself when told to do so, not to mention failing to go home before dark, not to mention failing and falling off the rock, yes, you could say there were mistakes.

Breathe through the pain, but it's the sort of pain that stops you breathing.

Do you really think this is going to work? asks the

raven. Have you considered the consequences? I thought these were the consequences, she says. Isn't this my come-uppance? Shit, fan, all of that? Police, fines, possible custodial sentence, losing the house, losing Matt, the whole village hating me. Yeah, the raven says, like that. But let's say you keep crawling, which is going to take all night and all day, by the way, you're not going very fast, and let's imagine you come off the moor and there's a field. What do fields tend to have round them, in these parts? Were you thinking you'd climb a stile? Do you happen to remember how many stiles you crossed on the way up, not that you're going down the way you came up, in case you haven't noticed, but as a starting point? Don't engage with this, Kate thinks, the raven's just trying to put you off, she's the voice of defeat, but there's the stile from the lane into the Breck End field, and then between the fields, and then from the field to the moor, and also where the path meets the coffin route and the raven's right, Kate couldn't get over, or even onto, any of them. Hmm, the raven says, and let's say you do reach a track and the track reaches a road, are you planning to crawl along the road in the dark? Though I agree it may be light by then. I've got my torch, Kate says, I'd be visible to drivers. She pulls herself again, gripping the heather. It's boggy as well as damp underfoot. Under hands and knees. She's not stupid, she knows how slowly she's going. Right, says the raven, and if it were Matt in this position, if Matt were lost on the mountain at night with a broken leg, query broken arm and a worsening headache not responding to medication, would your recommendation to him be to drag himself around until, well, until when, exactly? What would you say, Kate, what would your dad say, a responsible person in this situation ought to do? They might not be broken, she says, the bones. Not the arm, anyway. A stronger gust of wind pulls at her hood, spatters her face with rain. Matt wouldn't, she says. Wouldn't? Matt knows not to come up here on his own. Right, says the raven. And he knows that because? Because she taught him. Don't go up the fells on your own and if you do go up the fells on your own, tell someone exactly where you're going and roughly when you plan to be back. Don't rely on your phone, because there's not much reception up there and phones run out of battery, get wet or otherwise fail, but carry it in case it works when you need it or you come on someone else who does. Always check the weather, using the strangely reliable Norwegian mountain-weather-forecasting site, and always plan to be down an hour before nightfall so you have an hour in hand if you need it but also carry a torch because you'll feel bloody stupid if you have to call out the rescue team just to shine a light on your feet. Dad taught her, only in those days you carried flares and a whistle rather than a mobile phone, and she taught Matt. It's not complicated. This isn't the bloody Andes. The point, Dad said, is to have a good day out and come home without worrying anyone, but the other point is not to make a nuisance of yourself unless you have to. Sorry, Dad, she thinks, I'm so sorry.

She pulls on, nearly at the rock. So, the raven says, what are you going to do now? Would you have a plan B in your mind?

It hurts too much, and the hair-pulling feeling is getting worse, more like a scalping, a tingly soreness as if the skin on top of her head is stretching and stretching. Kate stops crawling and presses down on her skull until her neck aches, as if she could push everything back into place. Nearly there. One more pull, and another, dragging her hindquarters, she thinks, like a wounded fox, like a fox hit by a car and crawling to the hedge to die in privacy. She recognises the rock, knows now where she is, coming down the wrong side of the fell towards the reservoir. There's another tall stone round the side of it and a small hollow between the two where sheep shelter. She reaches out to touch the stone, hurts her neck again by tipping her head back to run the torchlight up the rock's shape to the raven sitting on top, its blackness gleaming silvery in the rain, the beak obviously a weapon. The hollow smells of sheep but there's no wind in here, not much rain, and she lies down in the sheep droppings to rest.

Someone's tapping her shoulder. Oh, it's the beak, it's the raven coming for her eyes, for her cheeks and her throat.

No, she says, no, get off me, go away, I'm alive. I'll tell my dad, she thinks, I'll call the cops.

Wake up, says the raven, you'll die if you go to sleep now. She curls the good arm over her face. We'll all die, she says, let me rest, my head hurts. You'll die tonight, the raven says, if you sleep. Oh well, she thinks, that way she's spared the consequences. And Matt, asks the raven. Yes, Matt. Poor Matt. But she's ruined everything now, hasn't she, she has no way of paying the fine, no one will lend her any money and quite right too, she'd have no means of repaying it. Her savings went months ago. And if she can't get home without being seen by someone, the whole village will know she broke quarantine, her friends and the people who think she's a daft hippy always making trouble about traffic and recycling and badgers and even telling other people to pull up their masks in the village shop, because it's not that she thinks it's OK to spread disease, it's really not, and it's not fair to Meryl in the shop when people won't wear masks, she doesn't have much choice about working there, and the older folk who don't want deliveries and don't do internet shopping and also run out of milk or fancy a bag of crisps like anyone else, they need to walk out and have ordinary exchanges with real people, it's not as if it's hard to wear a mask over your nose as well as your mouth for five minutes while you buy your bread and milk, is it? Anyway, she did tell them, more than once, no one else was going to, Meryl

always worried people will go to the supermarket instead
and everyone else just hoping someone would say something, well she's always been the one who says something,
someone has to, what you walk past is what you tolerate.
But now— she presses on her head again. You wouldn't
think it could get worse. The rock leans over her in the
torchlight, friendly, but she should turn off the light, save
the battery, and maybe it's the strap making her head
ache. She whimpers as she tries to get the bad arm to help.
The raven stands back, watching; Kate supposes a bird
could help but she still doesn't want that beak near her
face. Would you say, then, the raven asks, that you deserve
this, what's happening now? Would you say you've been –
well, sanctimonious, really, in the past, about the easy
stuff, the masks and the sanitiser and all that? Since when,
Kate wonders, has it been up to the ravens to decide who
deserves what, though it makes a kind of sense, as much
sense as plenty of other stuff, if the ravens are actually
watching us, keeping tabs, like drones or angels only clev-
erer, not answerable. Is she sanctimonious? Probably, a
bit, sometimes, if the word means what she thinks it does.
Some people in the village would say she's getting what
she was asking for. The raven eyes her, weighs up her just
desert, her comeuppance. Black eyes gleam in light that
isn't anywhere else, not in the muffled sky or on the rocks.
You're not planning to sleep, are you? she says. It's night,
Kate says, I can't go any further. My head hurts too much.

You were right, it's a stupid idea. It was stupid of me to come up here and stupid to keep going in the dark and very stupid to fall off the rocks and stupid to crawl away from the path and I can't see any options now that aren't stupid, and also I am very sleepy and there is pain. That's why you have to stay awake, the raven says, so you have two bad relationships behind you, you've basically run out of money, you've no job, you've no pension, you can't pay your mortgage, tell me another mistake, should you really have had a child with this man you never liked, do you think you've been a good role model for him, waitressing, being single, do you not think he'd have better chances in life if you'd taught him some respect for authority, but Kate doesn't care anymore, is drifting into the night, watched over by her rock.

another half hour

THE CAT HAS come to sit on the table and watch. I'm cleaning, Matt says, you've seen us clean before, it's really not that interesting, you move stuff and then you wipe where it was and then you put it back. He's not sure he's ever done this before, cleaned the inside of a cupboard. He's not sure how it's supposed to be useful. He stands up to swish the cloth in the sink of soapy water, squats again, leaning over the packets of beans and the empty biscuit tin to crawl half in to the cupboard and wipe. There are loose beans and lentils and bits of rice at the back because Mum never seals up the bags once she's opened them. The phone in his back pocket isn't vibrating, and though he's checked like five times that it's not on silent, it hasn't rung.

He finds the Sellotape, unusually in the drawer where it's supposed to be, and picks off the end, the click of his fingernail loud. It's been a while since he heard the helicopter. He bites off pieces of tape and closes all the bags, puts them back in the cupboard. He stands up, checks his phone again. Now what? Keep going. He opens the pan cupboard but it's really fine, there's no reason it should be wiped, it's not as if pans leave muddy footprints or spill their drinks. Cupboard doors, he thinks, handles, what are they called, high touch points, more to the point there are grey marks around them. Jake's mum and sister completely lost it in the first lockdown, went round bleaching the light switches twice a day even though they were making everyone wash their hands every five minutes and not going out at all, wearing disposable gloves to spray groceries with disinfectant in the porch. Jake kept sneaking out, mostly to buy weed, probably sometimes to sell it but Matt tries not to know about that, and then his mum screeched at him and then he wanted more weed. Fun times. You know Jake can come round here, Mum said, if he really needs to, if things are getting too bad at home, whatever the rules I'd rather he was here than roaming around getting into trouble. There wasn't much trouble to get into at the time, even for Jake. You mean, Mum said, the trouble's moved into people's houses, behind closed doors and net curtains, it's not that folk turn nice when you lock them up, when you can't see what they're doing to each other. Mum just doesn't like being inside very much, doesn't trust what people do in their own homes. That whole safe at home thing, she says, that doesn't really work for a lot of women and kids, there's a bunch of people who are safer at work and at school and out on the streets than hidden away indoors, and even if Matt doesn't think he knows any of them, he does, there'll be kids in his class, probably at least one teacher in his school. No, he said, no, I know who they are, some of them, anyway, everyone does. It's just luck, she says, if you're safe at home, pure blind luck. He wonders, sometimes, if his dad, or maybe her dad who died before he was born, some earlier man, taught her to fear those doors and curtains – so maybe this was always going to happen, her running away from quarantine and lockdown and the whole global project of confinement, but she didn't have to do it at night, did she?

He rinses the cloth. Clean the cooker, why not, it could certainly do with it. There's more sense cleaning what's actually mucky and the cooker is, a bit, come to think of it, cooked-on stuff round the electric rings. People do clean ovens, he's seen the adverts on TV, but Mum won't have any of that in the house. Ends up in the groundwater, she says, not to mention if the cat gets into it, though it's pretty obvious that cats have more sense than to eat oven-cleaner. He'll maybe see what he can do, if he hasn't heard by the time he's finished everything else. He checks his phone again, feels sick again. He could try Jake, get him to come over, bring some weed, ket even, he's not tried it before but if there was ever a time for horse tranquillisers this is it and it's not as if the police are actually going to come round, as if anyone's going to come and see him for real. It's not really cutting it, cleaning. He checks his phone again. Another half-hour, he thinks, another half-hour and he'll message Jake.

wrong side of the road

SHE'S JUST STARING at the ceiling, at the trees under the streetlight. There's nothing she can do, of course, no sense in staying awake, but she can't stop thinking about Kate out there and Matt through the wall here. What will he be doing? She can't imagine what Susie would have done at that age, or even Seb or Laura now. Crying and screaming, but you can't keep that up all night and anyway she'd be able to hear, she can sometimes hear if they're playing loud music or hoovering, not that it's a problem, comforting, more like, this year. And Kate, injured up there on a night like this, you have to hope it's only injury, maybe she's lost, it's years since Alice was up there but they say it's easy to get lost on the tops, rolls for miles with streams and bogs and those rock formations people are always photographing. She turns over. The pillow's all wrong, it's time for a new one, though who wants to buy a pillow on the internet, almost as bad as shoes and it's all very well saying Free Returns but you've still to have someone take the damn thing to a post office, more trouble than it's worth. When this is over, she thinks, emends as always because it doesn't do to get your hopes up, because it would be worse to live through ebbing hope and mounting bitterness than to expect little and set yourself up for a happy surprise, *if* this is over, she's going to go to John Lewis and buy new pillows, down pillows, and a silk duvet cover, and have a good long browse, homeware mostly because she has better places to buy clothes, used to have better places to buy clothes, King Street, not that she needs more clothes probably ever again though if she keeps gaining weight it might come to that. Lunch in the café with a scone and cream and jam to finish off with, and no, it's not that that's the best treat she can imagine, she's done plenty of imagining, it's just a little dream of ordinariness. Doing her own grocery shopping, come to that, nipping in to the deli when she fancies a pot of the good olives or some really expensive cheese, seeing something silly that would amuse the grandchildren and popping it in the post. Lipstick! A garden centre for spring bulbs, that particular sunny smell of compost and green growing, the wobble of a wheelbarrow when you pick up a rose bush and some tomato seedlings and it won't all fit in the basket to which you deliberately limited yourself at the beginning because you only went in for some more twine and birdseed, fine then so she misses shopping, so she's a shallow woman, doesn't the economy need people like her to go shopping, isn't it almost the duty of well-off old people to spend some money? And it's not all consumerism – well, not all material goods, anyway – she's also going to go back to that hotel in Lyme Regis with Pam, have a day in the spa, two days, swim in the pool, have a massage, feel another person's hands on her skin for as long as she wants to – two massages, or three – to be touched! – and she's going to go to the cinema and the Thai restaurant and take Laura to *The Nutcracker* at Christmas – next Christmas, the one after that, it's perfectly obvious how this Christmas is going to go, doesn't bear thinking about so let's not – even if Laura does think she's too old for *The Nutcracker*, Alice isn't too old. And she'll take wine to the book group, have them round here, light the fire, except that she's not sure she'll be wanting to spend much time at home, not for a good while. A holiday, Spain or France, though not on her own and who would come too? Not Susie's lot, not really, not for a whole holiday, it's sad to say it but none of them would really enjoy that, not unless there was a granny flat or something and she hired her own car and she's never driven over there, on the wrong side of the road, Mark always did that.

She turns over again. *If* it ends, and if not, then what, the last years of her life spent like this, locked down, locked up? Not that she is in fact locked up, of course, she could go out as much as anyone can go out which isn't much, it's only a recommendation that she stays inside, a strong recommendation from the government, but no one can go over the county boundary or meet another living soul and or go inside anywhere but a supermarket or a hospital. And there is going to come a moment, she thinks, not too far off, when she'd rather go out and take the risk, when the chances of catching the virus seem preferable to the chances of dying of loneliness, with loneliness, going mad here for the rest of her— stop it now, no feeling sorry for yourself, in your nice house with your nice— oh shut up, for fuck's sake, and it's not just about you, it's not about catching the virus, no one cares if you do that, it's about passing it on, it's about taking up space and time in a hospital bed, the doctors already sick and tired. It took her a while to understand it, after people being kind to her about the chemotherapy she thought healthcare was about looking after people but it's not now, that's why the nurses are burning out, because they can't look after people and the sick people are just vectors, naughty vectors. There was a young doctor on the radio last week saying that once this was over – at least she thought it would one day be over – she would leave medicine because people don't deserve her care, because they go out and meet other people when they've been told not to and then they turn up in hospital, hundreds of them, thousands, and the doctors work all hours but there are always more people breaking the rules and suffering the consequences and expecting help, and Alice thought, oh darling, oh sweetheart, if you want to treat only the innocent you are indeed in the wrong job. We all bring our troubles on ourselves, we eat and drink the wrong things and spend too long in the sun and risk our lives in cars and swimming pools, we exercise less than we should or play contact sports and ride bicycles and wear out our bones in the gym, we go to bed with the wrong people, trust them with our bodies and our minds and indeed aren't we sometimes the wrong people ourselves? Try paediatrics, she thought, or better yet the NICU, but wouldn't that be worse, really, to spend your days witnessing the suffering of innocents?

She pushes her pillow into shape, sends another thought out over the moors to Kate, wherever she is, whatever pain she endures. If Alice falls down the stairs, she has sometimes wondered, usually at the top with an armful of laundry, if she falls down the stairs and breaks her neck and dies on her new hall carpet, how long would it take for anyone to notice, especially with Kate and Matt locked up for two weeks? If she falls down the stairs and breaks her leg and doesn't die, how long would it take to get help? Three days, you can live without water, and in her madder moments she's wondered if she should leave a bottle at the bottom of the stairs, just in case, to buy an extra few days of pain.

This is hopeless, if she's just going to lie here and

wallow she might as well get up. Warm bath, maybe, a small and medicinal brandy, perhaps in another mug of the hot chocolate? Find something light to read, a Peter Wimsey or one of those, though she's read all the Wimsey novels rather recently, doesn't do to wear out your stories, she did that with Georgette Heyer, read and re-read too often until they were dead in her hands. A crossword puzzle, she still has last weekend's paper. Best not turn the computer back on, screens only make it worse.

She sits up and shakes the pillow, drops it back on the bed, lies down again. She does worry about Susie. Susie used to be more fun. Susie used to be nicer to her kids, at least most of the time. She was always a sulker, and maybe that's Alice's fault, maybe she should have reacted differently when Susie was little. She wouldn't do that now, keep asking what's wrong and trying to guess what to make better, rewarding the sulk with attention, but maybe by the time she learnt to let Susie stew it was too late, the pattern already set, a petulant middle-aged woman rooted in the teenager. Seven, they say, is the cut-off, don't they? Give me a child until he is seven, which seems to mean that however you fuck up in the first seven years of motherhood it's pretty much irredeemable thereafter and that's a pity because the mother also learns a lot in seven years only it's too late by then. A reason for more children, not to waste what you learnt from the first one, at least one child would have the chance to be functional though she can't say she's noticed that younger siblings are particularly better at being human than first-borns or onlies. It's not as if they didn't try for another, it just wasn't so easy then, IVF and all that, and they'd probably have said she was too old anyway and already having a child – but Mark would have liked a son. She used to see him looking at little boys with their dads, the clichés, football in the park which is stupid because he could and did play football with Susie and plenty of boys don't like football anyway, Seb, for example, not that Seb or any of them really seem much into physical activity of any kind and the whole lot of them fatter than they ought to be, not that she has much room to talk, all those cookies but she's not actually fat, just eats too much sugar which you can get away with when you don't eat proper food as well, at least as far as weight's concerned though you can prob-ably still get diabetes. Maybe she should get up and run up and down the stairs but really at her age what's the point, she can still dance, can't she, and not so badly either. That's something else for the list: go dancing, though goodness knows where, she's really not ready for ballroom dance classes in village halls. Tea-dances, score your cake at the same time. There'll never be anything like that again, will there?

Stop it, silly talk, no one knows what there'll be again, that's the truth, you'd just sometimes rather have dark conviction than the appalling uncertainty of hope, the risk of letting yourself believe there might be good times again, any kind of good time again, though on the other hand if you really believed this was it, all there'll ever be – well, people are born, live and die in much worse circumstances, aren't they, only not alone, that's the thing, she's not complaining about her material conditions. She kicks the duvet smooth over her legs and lies back again, pulls the electric blanket up around her shoulders. She's like one of those baby monkeys in the experiment, she thinks, the one in the Sixties. American psychologists took newborn monkeys away from their mothers and divided them between two cages. In one cage they could get milk from a wire model of a mother monkey and had a dummy cloth-covered mother without milk and in the other they got milk from the cloth-covered dummy mother and also had a wire model without milk. The great discovery was that with or without milk, the padded cloth mother was more comforting than the wire model, that the illusion of physical contact mattered more to the monkeys' development than food. The ones with the wire mother for milk still spent most of their time clinging to the cloth mother who didn't feed them but they went crazy and the ones whose cloth mother gave them milk were just very sad and insecure but not self-mutilating, and none of them, in either group, was able to reintegrate when returned to the other monkeys which really can't have been news to anyone and certainly not worth the infant monkeys' presumably life-long misery. Part of the experiment, if she remembers correctly, involved putting a robot that made terrifying noises into the cages to see how each group responded to fear; the ones who had to take milk from a wire mother had no source of comfort and screamed and rocked alone and the ones with the cloth mother who fed them clung to her. To it. She remembers Susie clinging to her like that when there was a dog or, for a while, a man with a beard, remembers that she must have been more or less good enough at motherhood to give the general idea of safety. Better than a wire dummy, anyway, as good as a blanket. She wonders if the monkeys' cloth mothers were heated, but she's not sure they had electric blankets in the Sixties and if they did, they wouldn't have been washable as hers somewhat unnervingly is. Calm, she thinks, relaxation exercises like the cancer nurse suggested, don't worry about baby monkeys half a century ago, goodness knows there are more urgent evils in the world than that, and she remembers a podcast she listened to yesterday about a German professor of medicine who'd tried playing people reassuring words while they were under general anaesthetic to see what would happen. They needed fewer opioids afterwards, that was what happened, turns out you can measure the painkilling properties of kindness, of the human voice, and when she heard the professor translating his recording she nearly cried. *You are sleeping sound and deep*, he said, *you can relax and rest, because you are safe now, and well protected. We are right by your side, and my voice will go with you.* Oh God, she thought, don't we all need that, surgery or not, don't we all need someone to murmur to us as we fall asleep that he is watching over us and so we are safe, though surely you need a real person not a recording, surely there's a better use for all this new technology than pacifying ourselves with a simulacrum of the relationships we can no longer have, electric blankets and recorded words of reassurance, cloth monkeys, that's what it is, because no one knows how to unlock the cage and we're all forgetting how to go back to the group. What if the surgeon himself said those words while operating, what if it were a true litany in the visceral real life of the operating theatre rather than wires in the patient's ears as well as on her chest and wrists and legs? Sleeping with that voice must be what it's like to believe in God, to be able to imagine – not imagine, to know – that this fucked-up world in which maddened baby monkeys are among the least signs of human inhumanity is still somehow secure in the hands of an omnipotent and benevolent father. Though I walk through the valley of the shadow of death, thou art with me. All shall be well and all manner of thing. Nice idea. If only.

She sits up, turns on the bedside light. One day, one hour approaching minute by minute, second by second, she'll be dead. In the time she's spent thinking this thought, the moment has come closer. One morning will be her last morning, one sleepless night, one waking, the last. A last set of clothes, brushing of hair and teeth. There'll be no more feeling in her skin, no more thinking in her mind or seeing in her eyes, blood will still and pool and darken, muscles set in their last form, skin begin to shrink. She will have to face the end just as everyone else has, her parents and her brother and Mark himself, who she thinks probably did know what was happening, just those final few minutes, the pain suddenly not indigestion at all, the fall, the last look of question and outrage, because even what they call a sudden death happens in time, must be endured, and how do you not know, how do you not think, that your own turn will come, that we all go into the darkness and end? How is that not frightening? Stop it, she thinks, stop it, but the truth is that the real reason she didn't shower, didn't see herself undressed or touch her own bare skin, is that there's another lump.

fairground ride

KATE CAN HEAR a heartbeat, feel it in the turf and heather, in the breaks in her bones, accelerating, louder and faster and nearer, in the rock. There's whimpering. Someone's scared. Someone tries to move but it hurts too much.

She moves off again, like a boat on a fairground ride, carried into the dark, though the pain is moving with her. A coin for the ferryman, isn't that what she needs?

A terrible light sweeps, flashes. Lightning, searchlights, burning her skull through her eyes, X-ray, brain irradiated, fused, fizzing, and the heartbeat again drumming, pounding. Rock, save me. Rock, hold me. Her body tries to curl up, to shield her head, but it hurts too much.

Kate sinks again, drifts. She's cold but it's all right. The shaking has gone now.

She hears her name. If I were you, says the raven, I'd be pulling myself together right around now. If I'd gone off and left a child alone in a house. I wouldn't just be settling down for the night under my foil blanket.

Kate, Kate.

Someone's looking for her. Searchlights. They're going to arrest her and she has to get back to Matt.

Keep still and quiet, between the rocks.

Coward, says the raven. Fool. You'll be lucky to live to regret this.

It feels as if someone is slowly pulling back her scalp.

rescue people

SKY'S CLEARING, STARS coming through. Rob pushes his hood down. It's almost like going outside all over again, having your face free, wind in your hair. He can see the outline of the hill against the sky, and the inevitable orange stain of Manchester. He wouldn't say he's enjoying this. You don't enjoy search and rescue, not exactly, not, at least, until a happy ending has been delivered to the ever after. But he wouldn't do it, would he, if he didn't like it, voluntary work, not only unpaid but actually in most cases undermining the day job. Mostly when people leave it's family reasons, which means their wives won't put up with another weekend alone with the kids, *you leave the team or you leave this house, it's that simple*, but if it's not that, it's work, employers sick of you being knackered and refusing overtime and generally acting as if it's more important to be saving folks' lives than going to meetings or selling stuff or whatever. It's one reason why he works for himself now, turns down jobs when he wants to, downs tools and leaves if he thinks he should, but he was never great with a boss, even Hamid at the end. He just likes making his own decisions, that's all, taking his own consequences. And he likes being up here now, feeling the strength in his legs and the heat in his body, pushing back against the wind, seeing the stars and knowing that down in the valley everyone's shut up in their houses, in their beds, breathing each other's air and waiting for another day indoors. You get off on being a hero, Liz used to say, you find it easier to go out there and rescue people and have them adore you and be all grateful than you do to stay in here and sit on your own sofa and talk to folk who know you. No, he said, I'm no hero, that's not it, you don't understand. I do it because I can, because we've all made bloody stupid mistakes in our time only mostly we've got away with it, so far. I do it because we all need saving from the consequences of our own idiocy once in a while. I do it because I'm not a hero, none of us is a hero.

All right, Miro, he says, rain's stopped, all but. Miro pushes his own hood back. At last, he says, still be claggy over the tops. Yeah, Rob says. They both know that since no one's found Kate on the way up, that's most likely where she is, in the network of streams and bogs and standing water stretching for miles across the high ground. People don't drown there, it's not quicksand, but they do get turned around trying to find firm ground, and get cold and wet and sprain their ankles and break their legs falling in the mud. It's a bugger to cross in winter, or really autumn or spring, at the best of times, which this isn't, and she'd know about it, Kate, she'd know where it is and what it's like, so why would she go there, with dark falling?

His torch picks up the Saukin Stone, after which they'll be merging with the other groups. I'll radio in, he says, looking like a long night.

Nothing, he tells Miro. Ann says Rusty went off up past Breck End to the coffin route but not much after that, too much rain probably, the helicopter's found nowt, no one else has seen anything. Line search of the tops, then, says Miro. And I'm supposed to be at work for eight tomorrow. I think you'll find, says Rob, that that would be eight today. Sorry mate.

They hear the helicopter coming in again, and that's when Miro turns to look back down the hill and his head-lamp sweeps the rocks and picks up a red rucksack lying open beside a water bottle and a packet of Fig Rolls. It's been there a while; torchlight reflects from rain pooled between its creases and some of the bracken has been rain-flattened over its lid.

checks his phone

MATT'S JUST SITTING at the table now, at the clean table, in the smell of lemon and vinegar, just sitting. He checks his phone again. Sleep laps at his eyes. He could give up, he thinks, go to bed, burrow under his duvet and wait for what tomorrow will bring, but he almost doesn't want to lose these last hours of uncertainty, of being able to believe that he'll hear Mum's key in the door and she'll walk in, take off her muddy boots and pad in her holey hiking socks to the teapot and tell him off for making a whole pot when he was only going to drink one cup, and she'll pour out the cold tea for making barm brack that she never gets round to and make a fresh pot. She'll scramble those eggs and make herself some toast and sit there with her hair drying in wild shapes telling him about whatever kept her up there, meteor showers or bats though bats hibernate, he knows that, and it's too cloudy for meteor showers. She'll be really sorry she scared every-one, Alice and all, and she'll somehow sort out the thing with the police, and they'll both go to bed and in the morning everything will be back to normal, to the extent that there is a normal these days, but that normal will do, he thinks, he'll take that normal, no problem.

He rests his head on his hands, presses his knuckles into his eyes until stars flash and whirl.

He checks his phone again, but it seems even Jake's asleep. The house sits around him, cold and dark.

This isn't going to be all right, is it, it's past the point where this can be all right. This is like the seconds between falling and landing, he thinks, you know how it's going to end and you don't want it to, all you can want now is for time to go more slowly than it does.

He checks his phone again.

He's needed to pee for a while. He should go pee. He should move.

Matt stands up, the chair squawking on the tiled floor, goes into the cold bathroom where there's Mum's deodorant in the glass bottle she refills at the plastic-free shop and her hairs wrapped around the shampoo bar and her bamboo toothbrush with its bristles bent. When he's washed his hands he picks up the glass bottle and throws it against the tiles over the bath and the shards tinkle into the worn enamel tub and the smell of rosewater and patchouli fills the room.

someone who doesn't ask

AT FIRST ROB thinks it's not going to be so bad. He radios in: she's a couple of hundred metres west of the Saukin Stone, downhill, near the stream, sheltered between two rocks and under a foil blanket which means that she was able to help herself as well as being properly equipped. Steep and rocky terrain, he adds, though it all is, round here. He and Miro hurry down the slope towards the heap of foil with dark hair strewn over one end and hiking boots at the other. Kate, shouts Miro, Kate, but the heap doesn't move. Rob can hear her breathing as he stands above her, rasping, not great, and when they lift the blanket the left boot is at the wrong angle, the leg deformity obvious. Kate, he says, Kate, I'm Rob, I'm here to help you. Her eyes are closed and there's dark bruising around them which is also not great, and overall his assessment is that they want that helicopter here sooner rather than later and also that they want to be ultra fucking careful moving this one.

Kate, he says, because hearing is the last thing to go, because even dealing with an unconscious patient you talk, you tell them what you're doing and why, you show the respect of one human being to another, Kate, this is Miro and I'm Rob, we're going to check you over, all right Kate, but we're going to be really careful, and then we're going to give you some pain relief, some very good pain relief. That sound you hear now, Kate, that's the helicopter, they're bringing the doctor to you, all right Kate? She's not responsive, probably not breathing well enough to chance morphine.

They put another couple of blankets over her, monitor the breathing, wait there under the stars as the light fractures the night again, as sheep bleat and run and the engine pounds the sky. The rest of the team is approaching over the tops. They'll have to get her out from under her rocks before they can pack her for the airlift and that's a job for more than two, with an unstable patient.

There's a bit of groaning as they move her, which is a good sign, and on the stretcher she starts mumbling. Rob leans in. Sorry, she's saying, I'm so sorry, I'm sorry, I'm sorry. He touches her shoulder through the wrappings. That's all right, Kate, he says, you don't have to be sorry, not to us. Her son, he thinks, if she comes through there'll be some apologies due there right enough, and she'll have to talk to the police, but this, he thinks, this is why he does it, because no one has to apologise to him, because when you've utterly fucked up and you know it is when you need someone who doesn't ask you to be sorry.

He stands with Miro, who has to be at work in six hours, watching the orange stretcher and the hi-vis doctor twirl up to the helicopter in a column of light and into its open belly, and then they walk with the others to pick up Kate's rucksack and take it back down to the valley. The clouds have gone east, the sky cleared, but the stars dim as they walk back towards the streetlights and headlights and traffic lights of the valley, back towards their cars and their houses and their sleeping families.

little dance on the dirty tiles

MATT'S STILL SITTING there, on the bathroom floor, when the phone rings. Unknown number, because God forbid they should betray a number he can call, God forbid there should be anyone to answer him. He watches the screen, the phone's jiggling little dance on the dirty tiles. He's very cold. He may or may not take the call. He might rather stay here, not knowing. He rests his head on his knees and waits for it to stop, and then he sits there, above his silent phone, sits against the cold radiator holding back time.

seed, breed and generation

THE RAVEN FLIES down the valley. It's hours yet, till sunrise. Sheep rest where their seed, breed and generation have worn hollows in the peat, lay their dreaming heads where past sheep have lain theirs. The lovely hares sleep where the long grass folds over them. No burrows, no burial. The Saukin Stone dries in the wind. Though the stone's feet are planted deep in the aquifers, in the bodies of trees a thousand years dead, its face takes the weather, gazes eyeless over heather and bog. Roots reach deep, bide their time. Spring will come.

sweet water

PAIN.

There's no weather.

The raven is gone.

There are voices, women's voices, and a chorus of electronic noise, beeping and binging, disharmony. Footsteps, the rattle and chime of curtain-hooks on a rail. The air is warm, stuffy as on a bus, and smells of bleach and school dinners, and under that of blood and shit.

Quite a lot of pain. She's on her back, leg uncomfortably suspended. There's a mask on her face. So I am alive, she thinks, is not pleased. She does not open her eyes, tries to glide back to the dark silence.

The air moves as someone walks past her, pauses. You can feel when you're being looked at. Swim away, dive back down.

The footsteps move off.

There's something in the back of her hand, inside the skin, sore. One of those needles, like on television.

She doesn't want it. You're supposed, she knows, to be grateful.

The other hand can move. She turns her head and the pain hammers. OK, don't move your head. So she is here, and cannot go, cannot stand up and walk away from the pain and the mess, from confinement and indignity and the consequences that are most certainly waiting. She lies still, does not need the raven to list what she has done. They fall upon her like a smothering cloth, her errors, the cost of her errors, and from the window at the end of the ward the sun comes out and its light rests on her closed eyes, shows on the screens of her eyelids oxygen in blood, the sweet water dripping through the needle in her hand and surging into the cells of skin and brain, heart and lungs and guts.

Life, then, to be lived, somehow.

ACKNOWLEDGEMENTS

I thank Prof. Ernil Hansen for permission to quote the work of his team; Dave Torr of Edale Mountain Rescue Team for allowing me to interview him and for reading sections of the book; Tim Leach for introducing me to Dave.

I thank my colleagues at University College Dublin for creating, even over Zoom, a good place to write and think: John Brannigan, Danielle Clarke, Ian Davidson, Anne Enright, Declan Hughes, Catherine Morris, Paul Perry. Thank you to the students taking my workshop classes, whose questions and ideas made the online life of 2020–21 worthwhile, and who met the adversity and disappointments of those months with grace.

I thank Sinéad Mooney, always my first reader.

As ever, I thank my agent, Anna Webber. It is a pleasure to thank my new editor, Sophie Jonathan, and all the team at Picador, especially Camilla Elworthy, Katie Bowden and Philip Gwyn Jones, who knew the poem of the hour.

In the US, thanks to my editor, Jenna Johnson, and all the team at FSG, and to Jen Carlson.

Thank you to the Brothers Gillespie, whose music helped me stay with Kate and who were happy to share a title, and to Andy Bates for the introduction.

All errors of fact or probability are mine.

The experiment with the baby monkeys was Harry Harlow's: Harlow, Harry F. "Love in Infant Monkeys." *Scientific American*, vol. 200, no. 6, 1959, pp. 68–75. *JSTOR*, www .jstor.org/stable/26309508.

The podcast Alice remembers is *Health Check* on the BBC World Service, broadcast on 16 December 2020 and presenting the research of Ernil Hansen's team at Regensberg University published in the *BMJ*: Nowak, Hartmuth, Nina Zech, Sven Asmussen, et al. "Effect of Therapeutic Suggestions During General Anaesthesia on Postoperative Pain and Opiod Use: Multicentre Randomised Controlled Trial." *BMJ*, vol. 371 (December 2020), https://doi.org/10.1136/bmj.m4284.

ABOUT THE AUTHOR

Sarah Moss is the author of *Summerwater*, a best book of the year in *The Guardian* and *The Times* (London), and *Ghost Wall*, a *New York Times Book Review* Editors' Choice and a best book of the year in *Elle*, the *Financial Times*, and other publications. Her previous books include the novels *Cold Earth*, *Night Waking*, *Bodies of Light*, and *Signs for Lost Children*, and the memoir *Names for the Sea: Strangers in Iceland*. She was educated at the University of Oxford and now teaches at University College Dublin.